DEAD FAE WALKING

THE PARANORMAL PI FILES - BOOK TWO

JENNA WOLFHART

This book was produced in the UK using British English, and the setting is London. Some spelling and word usage may differ from US English.

Dead Fae Walking

Book Two in The Paranormal PI Files

Cover Design by Covers by Juan

Copyright © 2019 by Jenna Wolfhart

All rights reserved.

No part of this book may be reproduced in any form or by any electronic or mechanical means, including information storage and retrieval systems, without written permission from the author, except for the use of brief quotations in a book review.

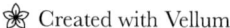

ALSO BY JENNA WOLFHART

The Paranormal PI Files

Live Fae or Die Trying

Dead Fae Walking

Bad Fae Rising

The Bone Coven Chronicles

Witch's Curse

Witch's Storm

Witch's Blade

Witch's Fury

Protectors of Magic

Wings of Stone

Carved in Stone

Bound by Stone

Shadows of Stone

Order of the Fallen

Ruinous

Nebulous

Ravenous

Otherworld Academy

A Dance with Darkness

A Song of Shadows

A Touch of Starlight

Dark Fae Academy

A Cage of Moonlight

A Heart of Midnight

A Throne of Illusions (Coming Soon!)

1

*D*eep within the ancient walls of the Crimson Court, a fist slammed onto a table. Said fist belonged to Balor Beimnech, our Master and our Prince. That was what we called him anyway. To others, he was the infamous Balor the smiter, known for burning his enemies to the ground. He was one of the most terrifying fae alive and had a bit of a temper, you could say. That said, his fury was kind of understandable in this particular situation.

Kyle, our resident computer geek, projected an image onto the far wall. He rubbed his temple, his curly red hair flopping down into his pale eyes. I could tell he was a little unnerved by Balor's temper. But Kyle was kind of unnerved by everything.

I, on the other hand, was pretty blooming unnerved by the image on the wall. It showed a handwritten note, scanned into the system for the Court's records. And it was not a pleasant note, exactly.

Dear Filthy Carrions,

A reckoning is coming. Your time of ruling London is almost over. The Sluaghs will rise.

It wasn't signed, but why would it be? Clearly, the writer of the words wouldn't want us to know who he was, or else we'd try to stop him. The Sluaghs rising all across London? Yeah, not really a fantastic proposition.

"Duncan." Balor turned toward his second-in-command, the leader of the guard team. "Give me your thoughts."

Duncan furrowed his bushy eyebrows and crossed his arms over his substantial chest. The guy was built like a tank and was twice as tall as I was, although that wasn't saying much. I was pretty short. Anyway, his massive size probably had something to do with why Balor had chosen him to lead the team of guards. "Sounds like a sorcerer. I doubt any other supes would use that curse."

He was talking about *Filthy Carrion*. Back in the day, sorcerers had used it as a curse to condemn supernaturals to a long, brutal, and horrible death. Usually, it was in payment for crimes. A punishment of sorts. But, as with everything, there were a few sorcerers who had gone totally mad. And they had taken the whole thing a teensy bit too far. They'd wiped out whole colonies of shifters, vampires, and fae.

It wasn't a curse that had been used for a very long time. For good reason.

I raised my hand. "Don't forget that I heard Fionn call me *that*."

He'd only said it in his mind, but still. Fionn was the Master of House Futrail, which was technically part of Balor's Court, but Fionn had started to go a bit rogue as of late. He didn't agree with Balor's alliances with local shifters and vampires, and so he kind of wanted to stage a revolt. So far he hadn't done anything more than puff his chest and make a lot of egotistical threats, but I assumed it was only a matter of time.

"I doubt Fionn would attempt to use the Sluaghs," Balor said quietly. "He despises other supernaturals, and he wouldn't be able to control them. Only a sorcerer could."

"No one in their right mind would use the Sluaghs," Moira cut in with her signature straight-to-the-point style. She tightened her golden-haired ponytail and scowled. "They're the walking dead. Sure a sorcerer could control them, in theory. But I can't imagine one would be dumb enough to get involved in that kind of mess."

Balor sighed, leaned forward, and braced his large hands on the table. "Well, someone certainly is. According to some reports, Sluaghs have been spotted in Highgate Cemetery. It's been at least a century since they were last seen above ground. Until recently, they weren't even seen *below* ground. Not locally. I thought they were gone from London, but they're clearly back."

A shiver went down my spine. Balor was talking about my run-in with the Sluaghs when I'd been investigating Ondine's disappearance, one of my only friends before I joined the Crimson Court. The undead creatures had shown up in the catacombs beneath London and trapped me inside a cage with a bunch of rotting coffins. Luckily, Balor had rushed in and saved the day with his fiery eye. Every single one had been destroyed. I thought that chapter had closed, but apparently not.

Shaking that memory away, I turned to Balor. "Do you think he's lured them back into the city somehow? Or is he raising them?"

He pressed his lips together, glanced at me. "That's what we're going to have to find out."

His single red eye met mine, and my breath caught. Balor was....well, let's just say he was the hottest fae I'd ever laid eyes on. Sometimes, it was difficult to think clearly in his presence, including now. I was pretty sure he was endowed with some kind of allure spell. Otherwise, why would I get so stupid around him? It was the only thing that made sense.

I wet my lips and gave a nod. "Right. Find out who the sorcerer is and how he got the Sluaghs back into London. Should be a piece of cake."

Everyone nodded and gave murmurs of agreement.

It would not be a piece of cake, and we all knew it.

"I need you to do something for me."

Ah, famous last words.

I glanced up from where I sat polishing my sword in the sparring room. Balor stood in the doorway, his tall, muscular frame filling up the entire space. His dark hair was shot through with silver streaks, and it fell into his eyes. Well, eye. Only one of his red irises was on display. The other was hidden behind a black patch, for safe-keeping. It held the power to turn the world into flames. So, you know, the whole patch thing was probably for the best.

"Let me guess." I placed the sword, reverently, on the blue padded floor and stood, blowing my wild red hair out of my face. "It has something to do with reading minds."

Yep, mind reading was my fae power. Sometimes, it was useful. Sometimes, it really sucked ass, particularly since I didn't have *total* control over it. Not yet, anyway.

I was working on it.

He stepped into the room, pure power rippling off his body like silky waves of heat. Balor was...something else. I'd never met another fae like him, and I doubted I ever would. Sure, other fae were impressive. But Balor the smiter was *more* than impressive. Every time I looked at him, I was struck by his strength. His magic. His bloody allure.

If only I could read his mind...but he had the power to block me out. So, most of the time, Balor Beimnech was an enigma.

A very, very good looking enigma.

"I do hate to ask this of you, especially knowing what happened last time."

"Oh, you mean when I passed out in front of the entire Court? Yeah, that was fun."

"This is different," he said. "I'm not asking you to read hundreds of minds at once. Just one or two."

Tendrils of his power reached out toward me. His magic whispered against my neck, so softly that I shuddered. Sucking in a deep breath, I stepped back.

"I thought you said you didn't want us to go there anymore." My cheeks were hot, damn him.

"We're not going there. I was merely trying to provide you with some gentle encouragement."

I narrowed my eyes. "Gentle encouragement, my ass. You're doing that bloody allure thing again."

He furrowed his eyebrows, just slightly. "Bloody allure thing?"

"Yes." I propped my fists on my hips. "You know, that whole magic thing you do to get girls to go daft over you. Well, you can just stop it. You made your bed when you said we shouldn't be a thing, so now you can bloody well sleep in it."

"I see."

"I see," I mimicked him in his British accent.

He took two large steps toward me, and his eye flashed. "Are you mocking your Master? Your Prince? Need I remind you that members of this Court must show me respect. Challenge me, and there will be consequences, Clark."

I blinked at him. "Are you serious? We're really back to that whole 'don't challenge me, Clark' schtick?"

"It's not a schtick, and we're not 'back' to it, as you say, since we never left it behind."

Balor and I had gone through a lot together, and I'd kind of thought that we'd come to some sort of happy truce where we didn't hurl threats and insults at each other anymore.

Guess I was wrong!

"Fine," I said through gritted teeth. "Just tell me about the mind reading task you're ordering me to do then, *Master*."

He didn't like my snark. I could tell by the way his

body thrummed with an intensity that made my mouth dry.

"You'll be leaving with the others tonight." All the warmth was gone from his voice. "I need you to read the minds of the Sluaghs."

"Read the—?" I shook my head. "But they're the walking dead. Reading their minds is next to impossible.

Just like reading yours.

"This isn't up for negotiation, Clark. It's an order."

"Well, if it's an order, then I guess I have no choice." With that, I grabbed my sword, slid it into my sheath, and stormed on out of the sparring room before I told my Master what I really thought. I didn't want to end up 'challenging' him again, now did I?

2

*O*minous bells tolled throughout the city. It was midnight, and the Crimson Court guards stood clustered outside of Highgate Cemetery's majestic gothic entrance. The metal gates that spanned between the brick walls were shut tight. During the day, the cemetery was open to the public, giving tours of the brilliant but creepy grounds to morbid tourists.

But it was midnight, so we had to scale the walls to get inside. One after another, we climbed the gate, and then dropped down on the dirt packed ground. Once we'd all made it inside, darkness closed in fast. Tangles of bushes and leaves hugged our group as we all stood staring in the vague direction of the heart of the cemetery.

I was not particularly thrilled about this mission, but here we were.

Moira, my closest new friend at the Crimson Court, rested her hand on the hilt of her sword. She had it tucked into a sheath that hung around her waist at all times. She looked pretty nonchalant, fingers lose, stance relaxed. But there was a sharpness to her golden eyes that betrayed the truth.

She was not thrilled either. At least it wasn't just me.

She turned to me. "Any idea where they are?"

"Um, no? Why would I know where the bloody zombies are?"

"You're the mind reader. Can't you, I don't know, hear them or something?"

I pressed my lips together and fought back the urge to roll my eyes. It was an assumption many had made before, like strange voices filled my head from every direction.

"That's not how it works. I have to be close to someone to hear their thoughts. It's not like voices just drift my way from all around the world. That would be crazy."

"No crazier than being able to hear someone's thoughts in the first place. Like, you can *get inside my head*. But please don't."

"Enough," Duncan said with a weary sigh. "No more chit chatting. We need to find the Sluaghs."

Cormac grunted his agreement. I sometimes liked to think of him as Duncan the Second. He was the same build, the same height. They both wore their hair cut close to the scalp. They always seemed to be together, always agreeing on pretty much everything. Only their colouring was different. Duncan was dark, where Cormac was light.

Highgate Cemetery was kind of massive, so our whole Sluagh scouting mission was probably going to take awhile. It spread across fifteen hectares on a hill overlooking London's glowing streets. We'd entered on the western side, which meant we'd stepped right out of the city and into a woodland full of stone angels and gothic tombs.

We inched our way down the path. The bulbous moon hung high in the sky, flickering through the dense trees. A mist hung in the air before us, adding to the whole creepy-as-fuck vibe. I fell into step beside Moira, while Cormac and Duncan led the way.

"I'm not a big fan of this plan," I whispered to Moira as the bustling sounds of the city fell away. In its place was an unsettling silence that sent skitters of unease along my skin.

"Me either," she said, and then shrugged. "But it's what Balor wants."

"And what Balor wants, Balor gets," I grumbled.

A moment passed in silence before she spoke. "You two are back to fighting, I see."

"He's so infuriating, Moira. I know he's your Master, too, so please don't smack me or whatever for speaking against him. But I swear. He drives me absolutely crazy."

Luckily, Moira refrained from slapping some much needed sense into me. I probably wouldn't have been able to do the same if the situations were reversed. There was this whole weird Master magic that we had to deal with when we joined a Court. Once a fae was initiated into a House, the magic formed a bond between the initiate and the leader of that House. And it made it next to impossible to do anything against him. Also, it could make you act a bit mental when you heard anyone else talking shite.

I may or may not have dumped a drink over a

perfectly nice warrior's head because of that bloody bond.

"One of these days, I'm going to lock you two in a room together so you can just have at it."

My entire body flushed with heat. "Don't you dare. We'd end up clawing each other's eyes out."

"I think you'd two end up doing a lot of things, but clawing eyes out wouldn't be one of them." She grinned.

"Honestly." Duncan huffed from ahead of us. "We're on a mission. Please stop talking about how you want to bone our Master."

"I wasn't talking about how I want to bone him. Don't pin this one on me," I said. "Moira has convinced herself, but that doesn't mean it's true."

It was true.

"Uh uh," Moira argued. "Clark over here is the one who has the hots for teacher. I was merely pointing it out."

"I wish Kyle had come along instead," Cormac said, ignoring us both. "He'd probably be shitting his pants, but at least he'd be quiet."

I stuck my tongue out at the back of their heads. Moira snorted. I turned to her, grinning, and she grinned right back. Even though I'd proudly spent the past ten years of my life alone and on the run, the Crimson Court was starting to feel, just a teensy bit, like home.

"Stop." Duncan held up a hand and came to a sudden halt in front of us. I almost slammed into his back, but I caught myself just in time. I craned my head around our leader's massive body to see what had caught his attention.

At first…well, I didn't see much. A couple of red foxes ran through the thick greenery, their bushy tails whipping from side to side.

Cormac held his ball of light higher in the air to illuminate the path. Just up ahead, a cluster of stone mausoleums lurked in the darkness. The path curved just out of sight beyond them, disappearing into even thicker shrubs. And then I heard it. The scuttling sound.

My entire body went cold. I'd heard that sound once before. Down in the crypts. Just before getting attacked by the Sluaghs.

They were here.

"Stay calm and get out your weapons," Duncan said in a low voice. He sounded surprisingly calm himself, which was just plain mad. The Sluaghs were no joke.

Steadying my shaking hands, I withdrew my sword. It glowed in the darkness, helping to illuminate the dark path. Balor had gifted me this sword when I'd first joined the Court. I barely knew how to use it, but I still carried it with me anytime I left on a mission.

Better safe than sorry was my motto.

"How many of them are there?" I asked.

Duncan's sigh was a whisper on the wind. "I don't know, Clark. I haven't seen anything more than you have. Maybe if you would stop asking questions and blabbering about how hot you think our Master is, then we could investigate and figure it out."

I rolled my eyes. I swore, he was almost as bad as Balor.

"I don't think any investigating will be necessary,"

I replied. "The Sluaghs will come for us way before we make a move for them."

Unfortunately, I was right. But as much as I liked being correct, I wasn't particularly happy about it in this situation. Who wanted to be attacked by vicious, flesh-eating Sluaghs? Not this girl.

Three of them suddenly scuttled around the corner. Long dark hair hung around their knotted shoulders in matted waves, and their skeletal fingers held tight to blood-stained swords. Magic pulsed through the dark cemetery, dark and cold and harsh. Dread skittered down my spine. These Sluaghs were nothing more than skeletons, barely clinging on. And they were coming for us.

On the plus side, their advanced decay meant they'd probably—hopefully?—be easier to kill. But...downside was they'd been above ground for far too long. How many humans had they attacked at this point? How many had they killed?

Luckily, these walking corpses weren't exactly the zombies of human imagination. You know, those scary stories where everyone becomes a zombie and the world goes to hell in a hand basket? Sluaghs were just the dead, transformed by some ancient, dark magic.

So, they couldn't spread their disease. They could, however, kill a whole shedload of people.

"Moira, up front," Duncan barked. "We three will form a protective shield in front of Clark so she can read their minds."

I frowned. "I don't know about this, guys..."

"Too bad," Duncan said.

"Tough shit, love," Moira added.

Dammit, I didn't like the idea of them acting as a

shield for me. I wanted to fight my own damn battles. That said, I couldn't read the minds of the Sluaghs if I were also trying, quite unsuccessfully I might add, to wield my sword properly. So, maybe they had a point.

Moira rushed to the front with her sword raised. Steel whistled through the air, joining the chorus of hisses and scuttling that came from the quickly approaching Sluaghs. My three fellow guards took their stances. And they waited for the attack.

Time for me to get my mind reading thing on.

With a deep breath, I closed my eyes. I concentrated far better that way, blocking out the sights and sounds of the world around me to focus on the invisible mind. It meant that I was pretty much helpless, but I trusted my fellow fae to stop the Sluaghs from slicing a sword through my neck while I wasn't looking. Their dark power still pulsed along my skin. I brushed it aside. I needed to focus. I needed to turn my own mind toward their thoughts.

My mind stretched out as my ears did their best to block out the sudden clash of nearby swords. Timidly, I reached and reached until my mind slammed hard into a wall. Gritting my teeth, I pushed harder. This had happened the last time I'd tried to read a Sluagh. Their minds were like shards of ice.

Ice that—

Pain lanced through my skull. I cried out, curling my hands into tight fists. Shooting pain raced down my face, down into my chest, until it spread through every inch of my trembling body.

I fell to my knees, my dark trousers becoming one with the dirt. Sucking in a deep breath, I pried open my eyes. My fellow guards were deep in the middle of a tense battle with the Sluaghs. They hadn't even noticed my scream.

Damn. I shook my head, trying my best to toss out the pain. That had seriously sucked ass. Last time I'd tried to read a Sluagh, the same thing had happened. Only it hadn't been quite as painful then. Taking deep breaths, my fingers curled around the dirt. The sensation grounded me somehow, even in the midst of clashing swords and singing steel.

Two more Sluaghs had joined the fight. Even in the darkness, I could clearly see a sheen of sweat on Moira's forehead. She was fighting for her life. *Our* lives. And she was doing it to give me a chance to read their minds. To find out who had sent us that threat. To protect our Court.

I had to try again, despite the pain. If I approached them slowly enough, I just might be able to slip between their mental defences, long enough to grasp a thought or two.

Gripping the hard-packed dirt tight in my hands, I closed my eyes again. This time, I reached out toward the Sluagh minds much slower. Two steps forward, one step back. Every time it felt as though they might have felt my approach, I slithered away.

Finally, I was there. As gently as I could, I pushed.

Stinging pain rushed into my head. My entire body felt split in two. I screamed again, the sound tearing at my throat. I couldn't think, I couldn't breathe, I couldn't do anything but give in to the pain.

Strong arms wrapped around my waist and lifted me from the ground. Duncan, most likely. Maybe Cormac. Hell, it could even be Moira. She might be more slight than the others, but she was still taller and stronger than me.

I let my fellow fae carry me away from the fight, away from the pain, away from the stinging bite.

One thing was for sure, I was not going to get any thoughts from the Sluaghs. The magic protecting their minds was impenetrable.

Suddenly, my saviour stopped and dumped me onto the ground. I fell with a hard smack, the wind whooshing out of my lungs. Scowling, I finally opened my eyes to glare up at Moira, or Duncan, or Cormac.

But...it wasn't any of them.

It was a bloody Sluagh.

3

"What the hell?"

I didn't really have time to process what was happening. The Sluagh launched itself at me. Its mouth was open wide, its sharp teeth glistening against the light of the full moon. The Sluagh's dark eyes were hollow, void of any light. It was as if its soul was a black hole, sucking every bit of life deep into the void.

Or maybe I was being dramatic.

It was just a bloody zombie, after all.

Down on the ground, I spun my legs in a wide circle. It was a move Balor had taught me, and it worked like a charm. My ankles slammed into the Sluagh's legs, and it went toppling onto the ground beside me.

I was still reeling a bit from the whole mind attack thing, but I still managed to clamber to my feet. Shakily, I withdrew my sword just in time for the Sluagh to jump back on its feet. It stumbled sideways a bit, and a massive chunk of his arm fell off. The two of us watched the broken limb *thump* on the ground.

It was just bone. There was barely any flesh on it at all. And, as I watched, the bone began to shake and crumble. A deep and sudden blackness swept across it, eating it up from the inside out. After a few moments, all that was left was ash.

"Huh," I said, looking back up at the Sluagh. "That was weird. Maybe you should go back into your hidey hole."

The Sluagh didn't answer, which was also weird. The ones I'd met in the catacombs had been pretty chatty. Maybe this one was too far gone for that. Which begged the question. Why didn't it go back underground? It was pretty common knowledge that Sluaghs couldn't leave the safety of the deep dark earthy places of this world for very long, or else they would disintegrate. And, while they were walking corpses with barely functioning brains, most of them seemed to understand that fact. They wanted to survive, even if they were technically dead. So, what in the seven hells was this one doing?

The Sluagh decided to answer my question by launching himself at me again, only this time his attack was more of a wobble than a jump. The lack of an arm meant lack of balance. I knocked away his sword easily enough, and then swung my own weapon to chop off his other arm.

The steel sliced through bone and let out a horrifying crunch. Grimacing, I watched as his entire body began to shake. That strange blackness bloomed in his neck, spreading out through his entire body. Two seconds later, my abductor and attacker was nothing more than a pile of black ash.

Wiping some stray bone char from my arm, I shot a glance at the empty path behind and in front of me. The Crimson Court guard team was nowhere in sight. There was just me, the pile of ashy Sluagh, a few scuttling leaves, and *a lot* of graves.

Well, this was fun. Not only had I failed to get a word from the minds of the bloody Sluaghs, but I'd found myself all alone in a creepy cemetery. This night was not going well, exactly. There was also the fact that I didn't have Cormac's power, so no glowing ball of light for me either.

I was literally going to have to flail around in the dark until I found my way back to the group. It probably shouldn't be too hard. They were running around slashing their swords and making a hell of a lot of noise. Of course, everything here was brutally silent. How far had the Sluagh taken me away from the group?

Too far.

Way too far.

With a frown, I turned back toward the direction I thought I'd come. The path was dark, cutting deep between thick trees. There was an ominous stone angel to my left. Impossible not to notice, even in the heavy shadows. The thing towered over me, its hulking form almost as tall as the trees themselves. I shivered and wished I'd brought more than just a sword. A chainsaw maybe. That would have made me feel a tad better about being lost in a Sluagh-infested cemetery by myself.

I ducked past the angel and pushed through the

thick brush. My feet slammed into a fallen limb. The forest was far too tangled for me to go through this way. With an irritated sigh, I backtracked and tried another route. It was pretty difficult not to scream bloody murder in this situation. I was lost in a cemetery, surrounded by dead people, and I couldn't see a damn thing.

Ten minutes later, things had not changed very much. The only difference was that I was now standing under a different stone angel. Maybe. The maze of tombstones and mausoleums meant that everything was starting to look the same. I was pretty sure that either my fellow guards had disappeared through a portal to another realm or they had left me here.

Just when I had decided that I might as well pitch an invisible tent to camp out in the graveyard for the night, a rustling caught my ear. Heart lifting and squeezing simultaneously, I whirled toward the noise. It came from just around the corner.

"Moira?" I called out in a hoarse whisper as I crouch-walked my way toward the sound. "Duncan?"

The rustling continued. It didn't sound much like the eerie scuttling of the Sluaghs, but whoever it was also wasn't talking, so that wasn't a positive sign.

Maybe he, or she, didn't hear me.

"Moira?" A little louder this time, though my voice broke on the last syllable. I was a little nervous, you might say.

The rustling stopped. Heart stuck in my throat, I

tiptoed my way toward the bushes. Probably a bad idea, but I needed to find out if my fellow guards were there. Look, I'd already kind of killed one Sluagh, so at least I knew I could take one on if I needed to.

A form lurched out of the bushes, faster than I could blink. I stumbled back, hands tightening around the hilt of my sword. My fear seemed to spark something in my weapon. A steady hum spread through the hilt, and the steel sparked with a luminous glow.

Which meant that I could now see what was coming for me. And it was...well, I wasn't sure exactly. Cocking my head, I studied the creature that was kind of shuffle-running my way.

He was pale. His eyes were dark and hooded, but they didn't have that weirdly vacant look of the Sluaghs. His dark hair was tied up in a man-bun, which highlighted his sculpted cheekbones and sharp jaw. He shuffle-stumbled a little closer. There, on his lips, was some blood.

So, he was a vampire. One who looked seriously worse for wear, especially if he'd just fed. Vampires normally looked pretty ethereal. Calm, controlled, icy cool. This one looked like a bloody mess. Pun intended.

"Yo, hold up, mate," I said, taking a slow step back when he continued his shuffle stumble toward me. "You alright?"

He merely made a grunting noise at me.

Hmm.

"Are you hungry or something?" To the gods, I hoped not. Vampires rarely lost control these days. Most had decided that peace with humans was more important than crazed violence. Plus, there were too many willing feeders for that kind of thing to happen anymore. That said, it did still happen on occasion.

Hopefully not tonight.

"Nrrrgh," the vampire replied.

"Okay." I wet my lips. "Listen. I'm half-shifter, so you don't want to go feeding from me."

One blessed benefit of my half-bred nature, of which there weren't many. Vampires couldn't digest shifter blood. It would kill them. They were allergic to the toxins, which meant they were allergic to me. It had never been something I'd had to worry about before, but my life had taken more than one strange turn these past few weeks.

My words went right over the vamp's head. He continued toward me. Now, I was backed up into a corner, and I was going to have to do more than reason with the guy if I wanted to get out of this thing alive.

With a deep breath, I raised my sword high. That seemed to get his attention. He blinked at me, backing up with fear in his eyes. I took that moment to take a prod at his brain. If he didn't want to speak, fine. There were other ways I could get info.

His mind, unlike the Sluaghs, was pretty easy to enter. There were no walls, no bite back spells. I just slithered on in as if I'd been invited. The irony was not lost on me.

The vampire's thoughts churned around me like a rough sea. I had to grit my teeth and brace myself, otherwise I'd only drown under the weight of it. This was weird. Usually, a mind's thoughts just drifted over me, word for word for word. Sometimes in bits and pieces but always one at a time. This...it was like a tidal wave.

Hunger, sorcerer, blood, kill, girl, graves, moon, fangs, need.

It didn't make much sense. It was like his mind had been messed with and—

That was when the vampire slammed into me. His body crashed into mine, his limbs flailing. Strangely, it was pretty easy to smack him back. I just kind of flailed my arms a bit, and he stumbled away.

There was something wrong with this vamp. His eyes were vacant. His skin so very pale. And he didn't seem to understand my words. His thoughts were jumbled, his body slow.

He's a Sluagh.

The thought popped into my head out of nowhere.

No. That couldn't be right. For one, Sluaghs were the dead. And while vampires were definitely magic, they were very much alive. Of course, he could have been a dead vampire...

That thought was crazy. There'd never been any supernatural Sluaghs before. They were terrifying enough as it was, not to add the whole extra powers thing into the equation.

But he was acting like one, and he certainly didn't seem like he was in total command of his senses. That said, he was definitely different than any normal Sluagh I'd ever seen. But that made sense. Supernatural Sluaghs would be a totally different ballgame.

"Nrrrgh," he said again.

"Right." I tightened my grip on my sword. Whatever this creature was, it was time to put him out of his misery. I needed to get out of here, and he was standing smack dab in my way. "Show me what you've got, Fangs."

He kicked me hard, showing a strength I hadn't expected from his frail form. I doubled over. My breath had been knocked from my lungs, and stars danced in my eyes. He was fast, but I was faster. All I needed was to—

The vampire kicked me in the shin. New waves of pain pulsed through my bones. Gritting my teeth, I grabbed for my sword, but it was just out of my reach. I'd dropped it when I'd fallen. Because of course I had.

Come on, Clark. Get a grip. Remember your training. Remember what Balor and Moira have taught you. Oh, and also, you don't really want to die in a graveyard from a zombie vampire, now do you?

With that thought in my head, I propelled myself to my feet. It was a pretty good move, if I do say so myself. Too bad no one was around to see it.

The vampire lunged. This time, I managed to dart out of the way. I dropped to my knees, grabbed my sword, and jumped back onto my feet again. Gritting my teeth, I widened my stance and stared the vamp down.

His eyes were more hollow than they'd been five minutes ago, his spine more curved. He was transforming further and further into the Sluagh right before my very eyes. Soon, his flesh would begin to rot. His bones would become brittle. Of course, I wasn't going to stick around and wait for that to happen.

Taking a deep breath, I whirled my sword toward the vamp. He tried to stumble out of my way, but he wasn't fast enough. The Sluagh magic was making him slower.

My sword sliced right through his neck. A horrible crunching and gurgling sound filled the quiet graveyard. Nausea rolled in my stomach. And then the vampire's head fell to the ground, thumping hard when it hit the dirt. Bluish black blood spread across the path. It was bloody disgusting, and I hated doing it. But it was one of the only ways to kill a vamp.

Also, he wasn't dead yet. It would take a few minutes for the life to vanish from his blinking eyes. I stared down at him, wincing as he struggled to breathe. I reached out toward his mind once again, my curiosity getting the better of me.

Die, blood, fight, kill, dead, walk.

And then a more cogent thought, right at the end. *More of us are coming. Viaduct Tavern.*

Viaduct Tavern. I closed my eyes and turned away.

Brilliant. Just what we needed. An Army of the Dead at one of London's most famous pubs.

4

I hobbled back through the graveyard until I finally found the crew. They were just finishing up with their own undead fight and were wiping the blood from their swords. Moira glanced up, her expression so full of relief that it made my heart clench tight.

"Thank the bloody heavens," she said, rushing toward me. She flicked her eyes up and down my body, then noticed the black ash on my jacket and the blood on the blade of my sword. "You alright? Looks like you ran into trouble."

"Had a little scuffle with some Sluaghs. One of them was a vampire," I said, nodding when I got a round of raised eyebrows. "Yes, it's as weird as it sounds. I managed to fight him off."

"Fuck yeah, you did." Moira grinned, pride gleaming from her golden eyes.

"Guess I've had a good teacher."

"You manage to get anything useful?" Duncan said, striding toward me. For once, he didn't look gruff or angry or irritated by me. Huh, definitely a first. Instead, he gave me an actual high five, one that made my palm sting from the force of it.

So, I filled them in on what had happened and what I'd heard from the vampire. They were about as excited by the info as I'd been.

"We better get back to Court. Balor isn't going to be happy about this," Duncan said.

Yeah. Understatement of the century.

~

The four of us returned to the Crimson Court. The massive brick building's elaborate entrance rose high before us, casting deep shadows onto the River Thames. Balor's Court was located within the old Battersea Power Station. He'd had it renovated several years back, and it had cost more than a pretty penny to transform it into the breathtaking home he had imagined for his fae. It housed about two hundred of us now, all in pretty luxurious accommodation. At night, my own room had a view of the flickering city lights.

We trudged up the steps and into the lobby. Marble floors spread out before us, as well as a red-carpeted winding staircase that led up to the housing section of the building. Down a long hallway in the back, I knew we'd find Balor in his office, furiously working on whatever it was he did in there.

Probably his plots to rule the world or something Princely like that.

But before we could head that way, Elise, with her smooth silver hair and clear bright eyes, hurried up to us, wringing her hands. "Ah, thank the heavens you're here. Balor's in the Throne Room."

My eyebrows winged upward. "In the Throne Room? Why?"

Even though the fae embraced most of the modern developments of the world, they clung onto their ritualistic past. Princes and Princesses, thrones, and crowns. The fae world still leaned heavily on that part of their past. That said, Balor rarely used the Throne Room, and I'd never once seen him wear his crown. He liked to reserve the expansive room for special occasions or when he had to make an important announcement to the entire Court.

"We have a visitor." Elise's eyes sparkled with excitement. "It's Maeve. From House Driscoll in Wales. She came to speak to Balor about Nemain. And Fionn."

Okay, so that was interesting. Fionn, from the Irish House, and Balor didn't get along (understatement of the century), and we'd had a little run-in when we'd been looking into the disappearances of several members of the Court. I'd poked around in his mind, he'd gotten angry, and then Balor had burned a hole in his boat.

It had been a whole *thing*.

"Huh," Duncan said with a grunt. "Last I heard, she was siding with Fionn on the whole alliance thing. She hates vampires."

Part of what had started the whole conflict was Balor's new alliances with the vampires and shifters of London. Now that humans were aware of the supernatural world, he thought it best for everyone to work together. Most of the fae didn't agree. There was currently a bit of a power grab going on. Balor versus Fionn, and Balor versus Nemain.

Of course, Fionn hadn't gone so far as to send in an undercover spy to abduct and kill fae like Nemain had, so at least there was that.

"He was kind of hoping you might pop your head in, Clark," Elise said to me. "You know, because of..." She tapped her head.

"Yeah, I got it."

"Alright, come on." She glanced at the others. "Why don't you all hang around outside the door. Just in case..."

When we reached the Throne Room, the door was ajar enough for me to slip inside mostly unnoticed. Mostly. Balor sat on his throne, a tall monstrosity built on a bed of crimson skulls. Every time I saw that thing, I was reminded that Balor was far more dangerous than he looked. All of those skulls? Enemies. Slain in a long-forgotten battle. Or at least that was what the rumor mill said.

Balor's single red eye flicked my way, and then right back toward the female who stood before him, with her dainty heels digging into the long strip of red carpet. She had short, dark hair that sliced against her shoulders. Her black, lacy dress hugged her curves, and her long fingernails flashed with the painted red tips.

I recognised her. She'd been at my trial, when Balor had first brought me to the Court. She'd sat by his side, waiting to see if Caer, the goddess of prophecies and dreams, would assign me to her House or Balor's. We'd never actually formally met. After I'd been inducted into Balor's House, Balor had whisked me out of the Throne Room before anyone could talk to me.

"Clark, welcome," Balor said, his deep voice curling around my ears. "This is Maeve, from Wales. Maeve, this is Clark, my newest."

Maeve shot a quick glance over her shoulder, sniffed. "So that is what your face truly looks like. Well then. I can see that it will only be a matter of time before Balor attempts to seduce you."

My stomach clenched tight, and heat filled my cheeks.

"Maeve," Balor said, voice sharp.

"Calm down, old friend." She let out a throaty laugh. "I'm just taking the piss."

Balor wasn't really the kind of guy who enjoyed having the piss taken out of him, but she probably knew that. And she was probably one of the only fae who had the guts to do it anyway. Huh. Maybe I liked this Maeve.

Unless she wanted to kill us all, of course. That might put a damper on my positive feelings.

As if reading my mind, Balor cleared his throat and said, "Maeve is here because she's concerned about what happened with Lesley."

Ah, good old Lesley. The serial killer who had attacked not only me but several innocent members of the Court. She hadn't gotten away with it in the end, but she'd left a trail of bodies in her wake.

Balor spoke his words slowly, as if they held extra meaning. And because I wasn't an idiot, I knew exactly what he was trying to communicate with me. Balor wanted me to read Maeve's mind. Unfortunately, it seemed I wasn't the only one who understood.

"Don't bother," Maeve said with a click of her tongue. "Fionn told me all about her power, and he gave me a few tips on how to guard my mind. She's not getting into my thoughts, Balor. And, if I'm honest, I'm offended that you would ask her to do that to me, after everything you and I have been through together."

Well, that certainly sparked my interest. Everything they'd been through together? Like what, exactly? Had they been an item? She was certainly pretty enough, and she had the dark hair Balor was so fond of.

Balor narrowed his eye, and spoke to me without even glancing in my direction. "Tell me you found something of interest this evening."

"Actually, we did." I didn't elaborate. Even though Balor and I had only met a couple of weeks ago, I already knew him far better than I knew pretty much anyone else in the world. He wouldn't want me to share the details of the mission in front of Maeve.

"Good." He gave a nod and stood from his throne. On the raised platform, he looked impossibly tall and commanding. He towered over us all, a Prince before his subjects. Not that I liked thinking of myself as his subject. Ugh, no thank you.

"Maeve, Elise here will show you to your room. Stay for the next couple of days. We'll have dinner tomorrow, and we'll talk more about your concerns." Balor strode down the stone steps and flicked his fingers my way. "Clark, come with me."

I followed Balor out of the Throne Room. He led

us down the dimly-lit corridor, toward the office in the back corner of the ground floor. When he pushed open the door, I was assaulted by, well, everything that made Balor who he was.

His scent enveloped me, a combination of jasmine blossoms, oak moss, vanilla, and patchouli. Thick books lined the wall behind him, old tomes that had seen many better days. In the corner, Balor kept a well-stocked bar full of gin, whiskey, and dusty bottles of wine.

He poured me a gin and tonic—my drink of choice—before pouring himself a Scotch. "Speak."

He was in one of those moods then. I never quite knew which Balor I was going to get. Either he would be this version—distant, cold, overly alpha—or he'd be almost the complete opposite. Oozing with heat, emotion flashing within his eye, softer, gentler. And when he was in this particular mood, he didn't like to ask questions. He liked to *command*.

"Well, it's a strange story, and one I'm not sure you're going to like," I said as I watched him take a slow sip of his Scotch.

"Brilliant. Go on then."

I tipped back the gin—liquid courage and what not—and explained what we'd found in the cemetery. The Sluagh, the vampire thing, and everything I'd heard from the vamp thing's mind. By the end of my spiel, Balor's eyebrows were just as furrowed as mine.

"A vampire Sluagh?"

"Yep." I took another drink. "I'm afraid so."

"And you were able to kill it?"

I frowned at him. "Don't sound so surprised. Is it

really that hard to believe that I could actually win a fight?"

"Yes, Clark. Yes, it is." But then his face softened. "Not completely. You did hold your own against Lesley, too."

Pride rippled through me, and I sat a bit straight in the chair. "See? I'm learning."

"Your fae powers are strengthening as well. Now that you're no longer Courtless, you should continue to see improvements every day that you're here."

Ah, the good ole' Court system. I'd never wanted to be a part of a Court myself, hence why I'd spent my entire life on the run, but I could admit that it had its perks. I was getting stronger and faster. Perfect for battling vampire Sluaghs.

Of course, I'd never had to fight vampire Sluaghs before joining a Court, so there was that.

"What did you make of Maeve?" Balor asked, setting down his glass.

"I didn't read her mind if that's what you're asking. She didn't really give me much of a chance."

"Hmm."

"I thought she was on Fionn's side. Why is she here?"

"That's a good question." He pushed off his desk and strode closer. I struggled to keep my face blank. Balor and I were now only centimetres apart. As much as I hated myself for it, my body tensed anytime he was near. That damn allure of his. "Whatever her reason, it's more than what she's let on. Her adrenaline was incredibly high."

Besides Balor's damn allure, he also had the power to smell things others couldn't. I still didn't understand the full extent of his power, but I knew he could scent adrenaline. It would creep me out, but my power was a hell of a lot more invasive than his.

I arched a brow. "You smelled her?"

"That's my power, Clark. Of course I smelled her."

One of his powers, at least. Why did he get to have two when everyone else had just one?

"Is it just adrenaline that you can smell or...?"

His eyebrows winged upward, and a slow smile spread across his lips. "A prince never tells his secrets."

5

*D*amn him.

A moment later, his smile faltered. "Speaking of scents, yours is strange. Are you wounded?"

He closed the space between us. My traitor heart throttled into next gear. Wetting my lips, I dropped back my head to look up at him, my entire body taut with tension. His silver-streaked hair had fallen across his forehead, making him look even more delicious than he normally did. And that was saying something.

"I'm not wounded. Well, I have a bruise, but I'm fine."

"Let me see."

"It's just a little bruise, Balor. Honestly, I'm—"

"Let. Me. See."

It was the command of a Master. Our bond cinched tight between us, a sharp tugging sensation from the very center of my chest. Magic pulsated through the room, deep and dark and bitter, like the winter wind. All I could do was bow to it, give in to what it demanded of me.

I hated this magic. It could be dulled with alcohol, as I'd found out from serial killing Lesley, but I'd only had a few sips of my gin tonight. I had no other choice but to give in.

But that didn't mean I had to do it happily. With an irritated sigh, I unbuttoned my trousers and slid down the left side so that I could reveal the top of my thigh to Balor. His eye sparked with fire, making my toes curl. He'd seen me topless before (accidentally), but this was a whole other level of flashing. If my trousers went even the slightest bit further south, he'd get more than an eyeful of my body.

"Do tell me," Balor said in a low growl, "how you managed to get a bruise that far up your thigh."

"I was fighting a vampire Sluagh. I don't think they're particularly discerning about where they leave their bruises."

His eye flashed again, and then he suddenly stepped back, taking a vacuum of hot air along with him. "Button up your trousers and go see Deirdre. She'll heal you."

"Honestly, Balor. I don't need to be healed. It's just a bruise."

"I will not have a Sluagh leaving a mark on one of my fae. Go get healed."

"Well, okay then." Slowly, I pulled the black material back over my thigh and buttoned up my trousers. Balor's eye tracked my every movement. He held his shoulders back. They were so tight with tension that he looked as though he might snap in half at any moment.

If he were anyone else but Balor Beimnech, I might think he was two seconds away from throwing me against the wall and ripping my clothes off. But he wasn't anyone else. And he wouldn't do that. For reasons he wouldn't explain, he refused to give in to what I knew we both felt.

There was desire there. As much as he wanted to act like there wasn't, there was no denying the lust I saw in his eye.

Which was fine. Whatever. I didn't care.

And if I repeated that to myself enough times, then maybe I'd be able to convince myself that I meant every word.

Once my trousers were buttoned, I turned to go.

"Clark, wait."

My chin brushed against my shoulder as I turned toward him. "Yes?"

"After you're healed, get ready to head back out into London. I need you to come with me to Viaduct Tavern tonight. We're going to discover exactly what is going on with the Sluaghs."

~

"Hey, Kyle."

After I'd popped in to see Deirdre—she'd rolled her eyes at me when I'd requested healing for a bloody bruise—I decided to pay my favourite resident tech nerd a visit. I was pretty sure the guy didn't sleep. He was always stationed at the computer bank, tapping away with his back hunched over his desk. Scattered around him were at least eight empty cans of soda, and a half-eaten box of pizza.

Even though the Court had a five-star restaurant on site, most of us still liked to sneak fast food in from outside.

Kyle sat up and brushed his curly red hair out of his eyes. "Clark. Heard the mission went...weirdly."

That was certainly one way to put it.

"You heard right." I perched on the edge of his desk and crossed my arms. "What all can you access in that machine of yours?"

"Um, anything?"

"So, old records from libraries and such?"

"Ah." He grabbed a can of soda, opened it with a pop. "Only if they've decided to make an online repository. A lot of libraries these days have gone full digital, but some can't be bothered to scan in the texts."

"Right."

He pointed at another soda and raised an eyebrow. I shook my head.

"What exactly are you after?" he asked.

"I want to know if there's any documentation of past vampire Sluaghs. I figured if this kind of thing happened before at some point, someone would have put it in a book. Right?"

He gave a slow nod. "Not a bad idea. I can start the search, but it may take me a few days to find anything useful."

"Thanks, Kyle. You're the best." I shot him a smile and pushed off the desk just as Elise shuffled into the command station. She wore fluffy pajamas covered in rabbits, and she immediately threw her arms around my neck.

"Whoa," I said with a laugh, hugging her back. "What's this about?"

"You, you idiot." She sniffled and pulled back. "I heard you got into a fight with a vampire. Or a Sluagh. Either way, you could have gotten yourself killed. Why didn't you mention anything when I saw you in the lobby?"

My heart pulsed. It had been a long, long time since anyone had gotten so worried about me. I'd spent so much time on my own, so much time separated from the outside world that I'd forgotten what it felt like to feel as though I belonged to something more. Something where people actually *cared*.

To top it all off, I couldn't believe I'd found it in this Court. It was the one place I'd always thought I had to avoid. And, one day, I might have to leave this world behind. In the meantime, well...it was nice to have a friend again.

I smiled. "I didn't mention it because we were all kind of preoccupied by Maeve's visit. I would have told you eventually."

A scream ripped through the night.

Kyle knocked over his chair as he jumped up. Elise's eyes bugged out. I sucked in a breath, tightening my grip on the hilt of my sword. I hadn't returned it to the sparring room just yet, not when I knew I was going back out onto the streets tonight.

"What was that?" Kyle whispered.

Another scream. It was coming from the lobby of the building. How did I know that? I had no idea. I just *knew* it, deep down in my bones.

"Come on," Elise said, marching toward the door

in her fluffy bunny pajamas. "Something's clearly wrong."

Kyle frowned. "But the security cameras don't show anything."

"Stay here then," I said. "See if you can figure out what the problem is."

Elise and I strode through the vaulted archway that led from the command station of the building and into the rest of the Court. The corridors were dark and quiet, and a finger of dread traced down my spine. Something didn't feel right, and it wasn't just the scream. A dark magic rippled in the air, so soft that I wouldn't have felt it if I hadn't already been on edge.

I pulled my sword from its sheath. Together, we inched down the corridor, past ancient statues of fae long since past. The curving staircase loomed beside us, the carpeted floors softening our every step. When Elise and I reached the marbled front lobby, another scream cut through the quiet night.

We whirled toward the sound to find a female fae with curly blonde hair, one I recognised as being part of the Court, standing over a rock drenched in blood.

Frowning, I sheathed my sword and hurried over to her. "What's going on?"

"That." She pointed at the bloody rock with a shaking finger. "It's the third one that someone has thrown at me in the past ten minutes. Every time I pass a window, another rock comes crashing through. This one almost hit me."

"Wait a minute. You're saying this rock was thrown at you?"

"Three of these rocks. All the same."

Elise cleared her throat. "Look."

I followed her gaze to find a smashed window, one that overlooked the River Thames. Cool air seeped through the cracks, and glass littered the pristine marble floor now covered in a smattering of blood.

"It just keeps happening," the fae continued, beginning to sob. "They threw one into my room. I got scared so I went to find Balor. Another one came through a window in the hallway upstairs. And now this one."

Elise and I exchanged a look. This was weird and also incredibly concerning. Two hundred fae called this building home, and Balor had worked hard to make it as secure as possible. That said, it wasn't a vault, and if someone wanted to attack this place, there wasn't much we could do but fight back.

"Has anything happened recently?" I asked with a frown. "Someone out there who might be pissed off at you?"

"No." She shook her head, blonde hair whispering across her shoulders. "I rarely leave the Court. I keep my head down, pottering around in the library. Why would anyone want to kill me with a rock?"

She sobbed some more, and I shifted on my feet. Elise put her arm around the girl's shoulder, holding her while the tears leaked out. Frowning, I stalked toward the window to peer outside. Who would have done something like this? Did it have anything to do with—

Another rock flew through the window, and this one came right at my face. I ducked down just in time. The rock fell with a clunk on the floor behind me and rolled several meters before it stopped. Streaks of blood stretched out behind it, like long fingernails stained red.

Heart hammering, I crouch-walked away from the window. When I made it out of sight, I stood and pressed my back against the wall. I waved at the others to follow suit. They scurried out of the way, ducking behind the nearest potted plant.

Right. Looked like I was going to have to step into an unwelcome fight for the second time in under twelve hours. No big. I'd be fine. I had my sword and my courage and—

Another rock crashed through the window.

I wet my lips. I might have a sword, but they had projectile weapons.

Didn't matter. We couldn't just stay huddled up in here and hide from an attacker, least of all one who had resorted to throwing rocks at windows like some kind of horny teenager.

I whirled away from the wall and stormed toward the front door. Balor joined me in the lobby just as I wrapped my hand around the golden handle. His hand curled around mine, and sparks shot up my arm.

"I will go first, Clark."

I wanted to say no. I wanted to step in and protect my Prince from harm, but his voice was firm and unyielding.

I nodded and stepped aside. He ripped open the door and strode out onto the front veranda, shoulders thrown back, power charging through the air. I took up a spot just beside him, Cormac striding out of the house to take up the spot on his other side.

"Whoever is out here, show yourself." Balor's commanding voice carried across the quiet lawn before it got snatched up in the river's wind. There was no response.

Frowning, Cormac and I exchanged a look. One part relieved, the other part eager to face off against whoever had the idiotic balls to attack this place. Balor didn't have a weapon out, but he didn't need to. He was weapon enough by himself. If anyone charged forward, all it would take was one single look with his hidden eye, and they'd be toast. Literally.

"I think you scared them off, Balor," I said quietly after several long and tense moments stretched by.

"Cormac, can you do a sweep of the outside premises?" Balor asked, even though we all knew that we likely wouldn't find a damn thing. Whoever had been throwing rocks was long gone now.

"Maeve is gone," Duncan said as he joined us on the veranda. "While Kyle was trying to track down what happened with the cameras, I decided to do a sweep of the housing section of the building. Maeve's door was open, and she was gone."

Balor's jaw rippled as he clenched his teeth. "Then, she's behind this. She and Fionn. That's the real reason why she came here. They coordinated an attack on my House. This needs to stop now."

6

"You alright?" I asked as I watched Balor weapon up. He slid a sword into a sheath strapped around his waist, but he also fixed two daggers to his thighs. He'd been eerily silent ever since Duncan had dropped the truth bomb about Maeve, and I'd almost been afraid to speak. Almost.

I was never *completely* afraid to speak. Such was the curse of being me.

"Of course I am alright," he said in that low growl of his that sent shivers down my spine. "I already knew that Maeve had taken Fionn's side. This wasn't a surprise. She betrayed me. She hacked our security system to take out the cameras. This whole thing was pre-planned. I should have seen it coming."

"You just seem a little on edge is all."

"Members of my Court have attacked my House. That is not only a crime against me, but it is a crime against Faerie. It is not something that is done." He grabbed another dagger and slid it into the small of his back. "I expected it of Fionn. I did not expect it of Maeve. The repercussions of her actions..."

He didn't need to say more. My grandmother had once explained to me what happened to traitors of Faerie. They were stripped of their powers and fed to the Sluaghs. Fun times. It was what would happen to Lesley after her trial and what I imagined would happen to Fionn and Maeve once the rest of the fae world learned of their crimes.

"You seem kind of fond of Maeve...?" It was a question I shouldn't ask, but I couldn't help myself.

"I have known Maeve for a very long time. Longer than I have known almost anyone else in the world. She once stood by my side when no one else did. And I have nothing more to say on the matter."

"Okay," I said, sensing how deep the cut truly was, even if he would never explain. Balor always accused me of keeping secrets, but I was pretty sure he was way worse than I was.

~

After we'd prepped ourselves and filled the team in on our next moves, Balor and I headed out of the Court and onto the streets of London. A car waited for us at the curb, shiny, black, and extremely expensive. Balor held open the door and ushered me inside. I slid across the leather seat without a word. Balor followed just behind, shutting the door with a click.

The car sped away from the Court and toward the bridge that would take us into the heart of London. I stared out at the dark river, at the low-slung moon in the smoggy sky. It was probably close to two o'clock in the morning, and sleep would be hours away at this point.

"I'm surprised you didn't send Duncan or Cormac to the tavern tonight," I said, finally breaking through the thick silence in the car. "They're your guards. I was under the impression you didn't get involved in this stuff yourself."

"If by 'this stuff' you mean threats against my Court and the entire city at large, then you were wrong in your assumption."

Right. So, he was still in a bad mood then.

"Do you go on missions a lot then?"

"I go when it's required." A pause. "In the past, I have sent others in my place to handle larger issues, like this one. That hasn't always been the right decision. Mistakes were made. I'd prefer to avoid making those same mistakes again."

I raised my eyebrows. Balor Beimnech, the great Prince of the Crimson Court, had just admitted to making mistakes? That had to be a first.

"What kind of mistakes?"

He slid his gaze my way, his face backlit by the flickering streetlamps that whizzed by the car window. "You no longer smell like a wounded animal."

"Wow. Thanks?"

"I'd like to keep it that way," he said. "When we arrive at the tavern, I need you to follow my lead. Don't do anything stupid, like go after a vampire who has been transformed into a Sluagh."

"You do know that I didn't *go after* that vamp in the cemetery, right? It came after me."

"You told me you wandered into the bushes calling out in the direction of a rustling noise."

I nibbled at my bottom lip. "Okay, so maybe there was a teensy bit of going after, but it would have probably found me anyway. I'd been separated from the others."

"Just be careful at the tavern. Don't leave my side and don't rush into danger. You'll be safe as long as you listen to me."

He shifted toward me and grasped my face in his hand. Balor's grip was tight, yet somehow soft at the same time. A chill swept down my spine as my body instinctively arched toward him. Call it the bond, call it the allure, call it whatever you want. I needed to be closer to him, despite the logical part of my brain telling me I had to back off.

"Okay," I said, swallowing hard. "I'll follow your lead."

He let go of my face, but that did little to calm my racing heart.

The car came to a stop a block away from the Viaduct Tavern. Balor and I slid out of the car and into the cool London night. Brown stone buildings rose up high around us, and the chime of bells rang out through the quiet city. Down the street, I spotted the tavern. Patrons had spilled out onto the pavement outside, clinging their pints of beer and having a cig. Tendrils of smoke drifted toward us. A metal sign hung above the red door, swinging in the wintry breeze.

I eyed Balor's very visible sword and then mine. We hadn't drawn them, but we were still going to raise some eyebrows. Humans were only just getting used to the idea of vampires, shifters, and fae living among them. Weapons were only going to make matters worse.

"Come." Balor strode down the pavement, wrought-iron lamps casting long fingers of light across the street. I kept pace with him, my eyes darting across every shadow we passed. Even though this place was perfectly safe, I fully expected Sluagh to lurch out of the darkness at any moment.

We reached the tavern without incident. Kind of.

A drunk human male stumbled toward us, tossing his half-smoked cigarette right at my heavy black boots. "You're fae. Aren't you? Those monsters who live in that old power station."

I pressed my lips together to keep from snarling. I really didn't like having a cigarette thrown at me.

"Excuse me." Balor strode up to the human, towering over him. Balor was at least six and a half feet tall. Maybe even taller. It was impossible to tell with him. His magic made him feel larger than life, magic rippling off his muscular body in waves. "We have some business inside the tavern."

"This tavern is a no supe zone," the human replied with a wide smile. "No fae, no shifters, no vampires allowed. So, just run along then."

Balor frowned and caught my gaze. That was interesting and not in a good way. This was the first time I was hearing that a place like this even existed, and I'd kept my ear to the ground when it came to London's supes and their relationship with humans.

"You do realize that's illegal," I finally said. "Discrimination laws and all that."

"Those apply to humans. Not supes."

"Step aside," Balor said with a low growl, magic pulsating through the quiet street.

The human male swallowed hard and exchanged an uneasy glance with the two humans who had joined him. "Right. Listen. The rules are the rules. I didn't make them."

With a frustrated sigh, Balor placed one hand on the man's chest and pushed him to the side. The man stumbled back, eyes widening. I rested my hand on the hilt of my sword and followed Balor through the tavern's blood red door.

There were fewer people inside than out. A couple of patrons sat on stools at the smooth oak bar where a frizzy-haired bartender was refilling a pint glass. Words were etched along the pint station, *Brewed beside the Thames since 1845*. No one sat at any of the tables. The clusters of red checkered chairs were empty.

I glanced around, searching for any sign of the walking dead. The red ceiling overhead looked like an eerie stretch of blood-drenched sky. Dim lighting glowed from low-hanging lamps, highlighting old paintings that had been lined with curving gothic frames.

"What can I get for you two?" The bartender called out before her eyes dropped to our swords. She frowned and pointed at a much newer sign, a lazy poster board covered in scribbled black marker. It said, 'no supes allowed'.

"You're not welcome here."

Balor flared his nostrils and sniffed the air. Well, not the air, actually. He was no doubt scenting the bartender. I took that as my cue to read her mind.

Unlike reading the fae, I had no trouble poking my

head into the humans and digging around a little. I kept my gaze locked tight on her face and reached out, stretching invisible fingers toward her mind. Immediately, I found myself inside, and her thoughts churned around me like a hurricane.

Need to get them out of here. He's not going to be happy if he finds out some fae came here. Maybe I should call him. They have swords though.

Her thoughts were rushed and choppy, and I had no doubt that Balor would be able to scent some fear.

"*Who* won't be happy if he finds out we came here?" I asked aloud.

Balor flicked his gaze my way, but he didn't object to my approach. Straight and to the point often put people on edge. And that was the point.

The girl's pale eyes widened. "I don't know what you're talking about."

"Of course you do." I smiled and rested my hand on the hilt of my sword. "You were just wondering if you should call him. I think it's for the best if you don't, and you tell us what he does here."

"Look." She wet her lips and took several steps back. Bottles clanged behind her. "It's not my rule. It's his."

I cocked my head and listened again.

I knew this would happen one day. I told him we needed bouncers.

"Actually, I have a better idea. Maybe you actually should call him," Balor said in a buttery smooth voice that would make most girls purr in response. It only seemed to heighten this girl's fear though. "We would love to speak with him about his new...rule."

"I don't think that's a good idea."

"He's the owner, right?" I arched a brow and listened in to the reaction she had in her mind, just in case she decided to lie.

He didn't tell me what to do in this situation.

The bartender's eyes suddenly rolled into the back of her head, and her jaw went slack. Suddenly, I was shoved out of her head as if a pair of powerful hands had punched against my mind. I let out a squawk and stumbled back, holding my hand to my twinging skull.

Pain lanced through my forehead, a sharp, stinging pain that I'd only felt twice before. When I'd encountered the Sluaghs.

I peered at the human through burning eyes. The girl wasn't a Sluagh. She wasn't even close to being one. So, why had that felt exactly the same?

"There's something wrong," I said quietly to Balor. Of course, I was being a bit of a Captain Obvious. Balor could clearly see that I'd been mentally slapped, presumably by the sorcerer, what with the tears pooling in my eyes and the way I hobbled with a hand held to my head.

Balor whirled toward the human girl, his eye sparking with pure fire. "Tell me if he's here. Now."

The girl shivered. She took another step back, and a bottle from the shelves behind her crashed onto the floor. She shook her head slowly, eyes wide with terror. "I couldn't tell you even if he was."

Balor stormed forward. "*Tell me.*"

"No, I mean it. I can't." She flicked her eyes my way, and something in her expression tugged at my heart. There was terror there, but I wasn't entirely sure it had much at all to do with Balor. She was scared of the sorcerer. And, suddenly, I understood.

I stepped up to Balor and placed a hand on his arm. "I think the sorcerer has her under some kind of thrall. I think, *magically*, she can't tell us a damn thing. He has her trapped in her own mind, and he just pushed me out."

7

"If you can't tell us, then show us," Balor said.

The girl nervously shuffled from one foot to the other, and then glanced back at me.

I gave her a gentle nod. Obviously she thought I seemed like the less intimidating out of the two of us. I couldn't blame her, really. "Yeah, that should be fine. Or down a couple of shots of that whiskey beside you. That would take the edge off."

"A thrall isn't like that," Balor said with a frown. "You might be able to numb the bond between us with booze, but this is an entirely different kind of magic. One that is much darker and much more clever in the way it hooks someone in. Alcohol will do nothing to tamp this one down."

"What are you talking about?" the girl asked, eyes wide. "What do you mean? What thrall?"

Balor took on this question, since I only knew half the story. "Your sorcerer friend has put you under a thrall, which means he's controlling you. Sorcerer magic is different than our magic, fae magic. We get our magic from this world, from the bones of the earth. Sorcerers get their magic from...somewhere else."

"Somewhere else?" I arched a brow. "Where?"

He lifted a single shoulder. "No one knows."

That...was a little unsettling. And curious. Balor had been alive for a very long time. He'd never told me his exact age, but I knew he was old. The fact that there was something about the supernatural world that he didn't know or understand? Well, it was surprising, to say the least. And I wasn't sure I liked it, especially since we were bumping up against the very magic he didn't fully understand.

"So, what do you want to do?" The human girl's soft voice cut through our conversation.

I turned back to her. "Just show us what you can. We'll take it from there."

She fidgeted with a drink coaster, obviously still uneasy with this whole situation. After a long moment of silence, she finally placed the coaster gently on the bar top and lifted the counter hatch. She scurried out to join us and then motioned us toward a rickety door in the back corner. The two other patrons glanced up from their drinks, frowned in our direction, and then dropped their heads.

When we reached the door, the human girl pulled a key out of her pocket. She shoved it into the lock and pushed on the wood. The door creaked loudly on old rusted hinges, like something you'd hear in a cheesy horror film. Only this wasn't cheesy. Somewhere down there, we might find the sorcerer who had sent death threats to our House. And he might be waiting for us.

"You can go down by yourselves." She pointed at a set of thin wooden stairs that had seen much better days.

"You're not coming down with us?" I exchanged a glance with Balor. His expression was pinched, his eye glassily staring at the human girl.

She shook her head, her frizzy hair swishing against her shoulders. "I don't like to go down there."

"Riiiiight." I turned back to Balor again. "I'm not loving this situation. It feels very 'it's a trap' if you know what I mean."

"Luckily, it's next to impossible to trap me inside a flammable building."

Oh right. He had a point.

"After me."

Balor strode through the open doorway and down the creaking stairs without a moment's hesitation. Taking a deep breath, I followed just behind him. We descended into a dimly-lit basement encased in cement brick walls. The temperature dropped when we reached the bottom, our boots scraping against the rough floor. Shelves of spirits lined one wall, and clusters of wooden kegs were pushed up against the other. A strange scent peppered the air. Blood and magic.

If it weren't for that, this basement would seem normal, harmless.

The door at the top of the stairs slammed shut, and the overhead floor beams groaned as the human girl walked back to her place behind the bar.

Shivers skittered along my skin. "I told you there was an 'it's a trap' vibe."

"Hmm." Balor scanned the room, clearly unaffected by the whole door slamming thing. Meanwhile, I unsheathed my sword, just in case. It was heavy in my hands. Sturdy. It made me feel a teensy bit better about this situation.

A teensy bit.

I would have felt even better if we hadn't just been locked inside a sorcerer's cellar.

"Hello? Are you back? It's about time you brought us some damn food!" The shouted words drifted toward us from somewhere within the basement. It was a male voice, scraggly but strong.

"Where's that coming from?" I whispered to Balor.

We were in a relatively small room with no way out but back up those stairs. The voice sounded nearby, as if it could merely be around the corner. But there were no other doors. Just four walls that hugged us close.

Balor strode over to the kegs and lifted them as if they weighed nothing. When he'd moved the entire collection out of the way, he pointed at a hole in the wall, large enough to crawl through. Huh.

"Hello?" The voice repeated, this time much more insistent—and irritated. "You can't leave us locked up in here forever, you know."

Balor ducked through the hole without another word. Cursing him underneath my breath, I followed. I had to sink onto my knees and scrabble through like some kind of animal. Who makes a hidden room with just a tiny hole in the wall? At least have some kind of door or something.

Bloody sorcerers.

When I stood from the ground and brushed the muck off my knees, I found myself in another section of the cellar, only this room housed five cells lined with thick metal bars instead of booze. I'd heard rumors about this place before. These were the old cells from Newgate Prison, once used to house murderers.

And now it housed supernaturals.

Three of the cells held occupants. I knew by looking at them that one was a vampire and two were shifters. I couldn't tell you how I knew, but I just did, like a certainty deep within my bones. Maybe it was the shifter side of me, or some new component of my fae power. I just *knew*.

The vampire was male, tall, thin, and exceedingly handsome. He had bright silver hair that he wore in loose waves around his shoulders. His eyes matched, though a thin ring of red wrapped around the silver. He was hungry. And incredibly mad.

"Ah, what's this then?" He flicked his steely gaze between me and Balor. "New victims of this arsehole sorcerer? I was hoping you were that human plaything upstairs, finally bringing me food."

I lowered my sword.

Balor strode forward while I turned my attention to the two shifters. A male and a female, neither as chirpy as our new vampire friend here. They both had reddish hair, muscular frames, and eyes that were dark with anger. They kept silent as they watched us watching them.

When Balor shifted out of the shadows, the vampire raised a perfectly-manicured eyebrow. "Ah, the great Balor Beimnech. I'm surprised they've gotten to you. They say you're the most powerful supernatural in England. Looks like they were wrong."

"They haven't *gotten to me*." Balor lifted the padlock on the cell, jiggled it. "I came down here willingly, to find out what the hell is going on." He dropped the lock, and it clanged against the bars. "So, tell me, what the hell is going on?"

"Ah." The vampire's smile vanished, and he brushed his silver hair out of his face. "Well, as you can see, a mad sorcerer is collecting supernaturals to turn into his undead army. He keeps us down here until he's ready to transform us into Sluaghs."

"Well, that would explain the vampire I ran into at the cemetery," I muttered to Balor.

The vampire inched forward, pressing his nose through the chipped bars. "You ran into one? At the cemetery? Did you happen to catch his name? It wasn't Dimitri, was it?"

"Erm, I don't know. He wasn't exactly speaking in coherent sentences."

"Tall, dark hair, fan of man buns, very vampy."

Shit. "That could have possibly been him. But it was kind of hard to tell. It being in the middle of the night and all."

Beside me, Balor tensed. He could probably smell the lie, literally. The Crimson Court had a fairly recent alliance with the vampires of London. If they found out we'd killed one of their own, even if he'd been cursed to become a Sluagh, they likely wouldn't take it very well.

"I thought you fae were supposed to have enhanced vision, like us."

"Yeah, well. I'm only half-fae." I glanced at the

shifters who were still pretending as though they weren't listening, even though I could tell they were hanging on every single word. "I'm also part-shifter."

Balor didn't react. He'd known from the moment he'd met me that I wasn't full fae, even if I'd never voiced it aloud to him. And he didn't care, even though others might. To him, I was fae and that was that.

The shifters in the cell began to stir. They probably wondered what kind of shifter I was, and what I could do. Truth was, I didn't know myself. I'd never transformed into an animal, probably because I'd never tried.

The vampire let out a hollow laugh. "No wonder she's in your Court. You're the only one who won't try to stamp out the animal inside of her."

I cleared my throat. "Anyway. We should probably get you all out of here. Make like a tree, leave, and all that jazz. I have a feeling the bartender has made a call to a certain sorcerer. I doubt we have much time before he gets here."

"You're right," the vampire said. "She's under some kind of thrall. She and some others. From what I could hear, the sorcerer has promised them to be the 'chosen few' who will be protected and not turned into Sluaghs during the supernatural apocalypse."

Well, that kind of explained her loyalty, though I couldn't imagine turning my back against humanity, even if someone promised me protection. Not to mention that the sorcerer had probably flat-out lied to them. He wasn't going to protect some random humans. He would use them to get what he wanted, and then poof. They'd get turned into Sluaghs, too.

"Right. Stand back," Balor ordered.

The vampire lifted a brow, crossed his arms over his chest, and shook his head. "Don't tell me you're going to use that infamous eye of yours."

"You bloody well believe that's what I'm going to do. Now, stand back."

The vampire clucked his tongue. "I don't think so. While I would like nothing more than to see your flaming eye in its full glory, fire is one of the only things that can kill me. I would prefer not to end this night as a pile of ash."

"You don't have a choice," Balor said in a low growl. "You can either stand back and let me break you out of here, or you can stay to get turned into a Sluagh by the sorcerer. And then we'll have to kill you."

Shivers coursed along my skin. Balor could be...well, terrifying. And kind of moody, if I was being honest. I kind of understood the vampire's point. This didn't look like a great place to let forth a ton of fire. There was a lot of booze through the hole in the wall. Too many flames, and this entire place could explode.

I placed a gentle hand on Balor's arm. "Maybe there's another—"

Balor shook off my hand but didn't even turn to look me in the eye. I hated when he did this. He became the monster—the cold, dominant arsehole he wanted everyone to believe he was. I'd seen another side of him, only briefly. I knew it was there. I knew he liked to keep it hidden from the world. But that didn't mean it didn't hurt when he pushed me away.

"This is the only way for all of us to get out of here."

The vampire frowned, and his eyes pinched inward. "Okay, but if you burn me to a crisp, I swear to the gods that I will come back and haunt you for the rest of your bloody life."

The vampire stepped back, and so did the shifters. They pushed up against the far walls of the cell, frowning out at Balor whose temper was growing with every beat that passed. Finally, Balor lifted his eye patch to reveal himself in all his terrifying glory.

His eyes glowed red. Sucking in a sharp breath, I stumbled away from him. And then he let loose the fire from his soul. Flames rushed from within him, a gust of pure fire that exploded from his open eye as if it were the mouth of a dragon. Heat soared along my skin as the fire built into a roaring crescendo. The flames licked the walls, engulfing everything in sight, including the cells.

Smoke filled my eyes and my lungs. I ducked low to the ground, peering through the blackened cellar. Gates clanged as Balor ripped the doors from the cell walls. The vampire and the shifters spilled out into the room, coughing and blinking against the smoke.

And then Balor turned his eye onto the ceiling above.

8

The five of us managed to get out of the cellar in one piece. Barely. Balor burned a hole in the ceiling, and he and the vampire helped the more vertically challenged of us scrabble through the smoking ruins. They followed close behind me and the other shifters, the heat of the inferno seeping through the floorboards.

When we got outside, we found humans screaming and rushing away from the bar as fast as they could go. The vampire's eyes lit up, he sniffed the air, and then he was off, disappearing through the thick smoke.

I stumbled out onto the pavement, coughing and looking for any sign of the vamp. He was hungry, angry, but he was far too fast for me to catch. The shifters had disappeared in the chaos, not that I could blame them. It was just me and Balor again. For once, I wasn't particularly happy about that fact.

The car screeched up to the curb, and we both fell inside. We were silent for quite a long time, until the flames disappeared from the view through the rear window. Sirens peppered the night as cars squealed down the street past ours. Other than that, it was far too quiet, far too calm.

Finally, I cut my eyes toward him, my voice sharp. "Aren't you going to do something about that?"

"The human authorities will extinguish the fire. The vampire was hungry, but he did not attack anyone on his way to the blood bank." No emotion. No nothing. He was like a wall of pure ice.

Funny, since he was practically made of fire.

"I thought you didn't like to cause trouble. I thought you liked keeping the peace. You just burned down an entire building in the middle of London. When humans were inside of it."

"The two humans inside of the bar left before the fire started. The ones outside who taunted us ran away," he replied in a crisp voice. "As for the girl under the sorcerer's thrall, she got out safely. I could scent her fear as she fled."

"You know, sometimes I really don't understand you at all. Stop the car."

The driver up front ignored me, and the wheels kept spinning along the slick pavement.

"Stop the car," I said again, this time louder.

But the driver wouldn't stop the car, and I knew it. Not unless Balor gave the order, which he definitely wasn't going to do. And, if I tried to jump out of the moving vehicle, he would likely give an order for me to stop.

It was useless trying to fight against him.

And it made me bloody mad.

"What exactly do you think you'll accomplish if you get out of the car, Clark?"

"I want to go help stop the fire," I said, throwing up my hands. "Before anyone gets hurt. Why don't you understand that?"

"And how do you plan to stop the fire? Do you not think the humans are better equipped for the job, with their hoses and their water and their trucks?"

I glared at him. I hated that he made sense, because all I wanted to do was argue with him. "You shouldn't have burned down the building."

He turned away, his sharp jaw illuminated by passing streetlamps. "I saw no other way to get the prisoners out of the cellar. If we had left them there, the sorcerer would have sentenced them to long and brutal deaths as Sluaghs. They might not be a part of this Court, but the supernaturals of this city are still my responsibility."

Huffing, I turned away. Clearly, he couldn't see why I was angry about what he did. He was an ancient fae. A Prince and a Master. He'd never lived amongst the humans, like I had. He couldn't see things the same way I could.

"I don't think you understand how terrifying you can be," I finally said, in a soft voice. "Your fire...it consumes everything. I've never seen anything like it."

"You fear my power?" Something in his voice made me shift my gaze from outside and back onto his face.

"I mean, yeah. Doesn't everyone?"

His expression went tight. "And so you fear me?"

"A little," I admitted. "I think anyone who has seen your power would feel a little out-of-sorts about it."

"I see." He let out a hollow sigh. "To be honest,

Clark, I did not think you would be afraid of me. It's the last thing I want."

~

The next morning, I got up at six. Before I'd joined the Court, dawn and I rarely saw eye-to-eye. I was more of a night owl kind of girl, but days at the Crimson Court started early. There was extra training that I managed to get in by myself, followed by a short breakfast, and then long days in the command station. After last night's excursions, I'd only had a couple of hours of sleep, but we had a meeting right at nine.

And Balor hated when anyone was late.

When I stepped into the sparring room, Moira was waiting for me. Her golden hair was held back in a tight ponytail, highlighting the angular features of her face. She grinned until she saw the look in my eye.

"Uh oh, what's Mr. Grumps done now?"

Balor would be pissed if he knew that Moira and Elise had taken to calling him Mr. Grumps, but I'd never tell.

I sighed and kicked off my shoes before jumping onto the blue padded floor. "He's just being Balor, which shouldn't upset me."

"But it does." She lifted an eyebrow. "What did he do, Clark?"

"He burned down a building in the middle of London, with humans around." I took my sword in my hands, twirled the hilt between my fingers. "And then he acted annoyed when I tried talking to him about it."

"Ah." Her lips curled into a smile. "Was it really talking or did you do a bit of your snarky arguing thing?"

"Someone could have gotten hurt, Moira."

"But no one did." She strode over to her backpack, pulled out a newspaper, and tossed it my way. On the front page, there was an article about the fire. Only the bar had burned down. None of the other buildings around it had caught aflame. And they hadn't found any bodies within the remains. Yet.

Unfortunately, all was not well. The article pointed out that supernaturals had been seen in the area by an eyewitness named Susanna. They had a photo of her beside the quote. It was the frizzy-haired bartender who was enthralled by the sorcerer.

I tapped the paper, looked up at Moira. "Okay, so no one died, but this isn't good."

"It's not ideal, but we've had worse. The human press has had it out for us for a long time now. One tiny little article won't do any more damage than has already been done."

"Hmm." Moira might be right, but I still had a bad feeling about it. In the past ten years that supernaturals had come out to the wider world, tensions had been high. Humans hadn't made much of a move against us, solely because we'd been on our best behaviour in order to keep the peace. Vampires, for the most part, didn't feed on innocents anymore. They had turned to blood bags and volunteers for their food. And shifters just liked to stick to themselves.

Peace was uneasy, but it was still peace.

If humans started to feel that the danger was real, things would most certainly change.

9

"You're not going to believe who's here." Elise rushed up to me, her eyes sparkling.

I slowed when I turned the corner and my eyes locked on a very familiar, very fit face. My feet stumbled just a bit. I hadn't expected to see him again. Not for awhile, at least. He'd returned to his own House after we had defeated Lesley, half-broken from the number of times she had stopped his heart. A House that wasn't particularly fond of mine at the moment.

It was Tiarnan.

His lips twisted into a genuine smile when he spotted me across the lobby, the overhead chandelier catching on the highlights in his dark, wavy hair. His jaw was sharp and angular, but there was a boyishness to his expression that made him look a lot more open and relaxed than Balor ever did.

They were pretty much total opposites. If I was honest, that was kind of what I liked about him.

"Clark." His grin widened and he motioned me to

join him in the lobby. "You look shocked to see me. Hopefully not in a bad way?"

Another point in the Tiarnan column. He didn't have Balor's overinflated ego.

"Tiarnan? I...why are you—" I could barely think straight, let alone voice my muddled thoughts out loud. I stopped myself, then tried again. "It's good to see you. I'm just surprised you're here. I figured Fionn would have forbidden you from ever coming here again, what with the whole..."

"The whole boat burning thing." He flicked his eyes toward Moira and Elise. "Yeah, he's still not happy about that."

I strode closer to him, my boots clacking against the smooth marble floor of the lobby. Everything here was shiny and new, and it had almost blinded me when I'd first arrived at the Court. I was slowly getting used to it now, even if I often felt like I was walking on glass.

"So, what's the story?" I asked. "Did Fionn send you to tell us all to bugger off?"

Tiarnan glanced away and cleared his throat. "Not exactly. He's still angry that I worked with you on the Lesley case. He hasn't banished me exactly, but he's not letting me back into the House right now. So, I have nowhere to live at the moment. I came to ask Balor if I could stay in London…it might not be my House, but it is my Court."

Ouch. That had to suck. Tiarnan had fought by Fionn's side for years. He was part of his exalted Fianna. To discover he wasn't welcome there anymore…that had to hit him where it hurt.

"I'm sorry. This is partly my fault. If you hadn't helped me, then you wouldn't be in this mess."

"It was my fault for investigating Fionn in the first place."

"Maybe so, but..." I lifted my shoulders in a shrug. "I'm sorry. Luckily, I'm sure Balor will let you stay here until you work things out with Fionn. Although you do understand that he might take that as a further slight? Fionn isn't particularly fond of any of us right now."

"If he does, then so be it. I can just stay here. I'm pretty fond of this House. And the fae within it."

My cheeks flamed. His gaze was warm and smooth, and I couldn't help but think that maybe things could have been different if we'd met in better circumstances. He was a nice, strong fae warrior. Much nicer than most males I'd ever met. And he was interested in me. That much he'd made very clear.

But he was part of a rival House. He might be in London for now, but I imagined it wouldn't be for very long. He was one of Fionn's strongest fighters. The Master of House Futrail would want him back.

Footsteps sounded on the floor. I didn't need to turn around to know who was there. Balor's power and presence washed over me, and the deep scent of him drifted into my nose: jasmine, oak, and vanilla. I knew my expression must have changed, despite my every attempt to keep it blank. Tiarnan's eyes widened when he saw the look on my face, and then he stepped away. Almost like he was disappointed.

"I'm not sure which of my guards let a Fianna through the front doors, but they will be dealt with." His words were directed toward me. The warmth in my cheeks deepened. "Tiarnan, explain yourself. After the recent attack on this Court, I do find it suspect that you are here now, especially after everything that has happened between our Houses."

"My Prince." Tiarnan lowered his head just slightly. "I can assure you that I had nothing to do with the recent attack on this Court. Shall we chat in private?"

"No," Balor said in a low growl. "We will chat here in front of my team of guards."

"Right." Tiarnan shot me a look. I merely shrugged. Balor was being a little harsh, but I couldn't blame him for once. I knew that Tiarnan would never attack the Court. He was much too honourable for that. But his timing would cause Balor to be suspicious, and it was Balor's job to be suspicious.

Two hundred fae depended on him to be just that.

Tiarnan quickly explained what he'd already mentioned to me, with a few added details about the state of Fionn's mood. Apparently, Fionn had let him back inside the House, only for him to kick Tiarnan right back out again. He was convinced that Tiarnan had lost his honour, that he had no place in the Fianna anymore.

"So, you wish to stay here, temporarily. And then you wish to return to your old Master, who wants nothing more than to see me lose my power over this Court?" Balor lifted an eyebrow. "That is a fairly large ask, Tiarnan. Even for a Fianna."

"I'm not entirely sure I wish to return to my House. All I know is that I am part of the Crimson Court, and I currently have no home. Initiate me as a new member of your House if you must. Just please do not turn me away like Fionn did."

"Hmm." Balor turned toward Elise. "Your thoughts."

"I understand your hesitation, but he has nowhere to go. And he's right. This is his Court..."

Then, Balor turned toward me. "Read his mind. I need you to make certain that he is genuine in his request."

Ugh. I hated when he did this. Using my power as some kind of advanced interrogation technique had never been high on my list of fun things to do. I'd told him—repeatedly—that I didn't like using my power this way. It felt more like an intrusion than it did when I was more subtle about it.

Besides, this was Tiarnan we were talking about. He was my friend.

With a heavy sigh, Tiarnan shifted my way and searched my eyes with his. "You going to go digging around in my head again then?"

My heart throbbed. I could tell by the look in his eye and the tone of his voice that if I did this, any possibility of something happening between us would be one hundred percent over. And I couldn't blame him. I'd read his mind a couple of times, right when we'd met, but I'd held back since then. Over the years, I'd read the minds of friends far too often. It always ended in heartache. Besides, of all the fae I'd ever met, Tiarnan didn't deserve someone poking around in his brain, particularly someone he was interested in.

Even if I hesitated when it came to pursuing something with him, I hated the idea of slamming the door shut on it forever. Of ruining any friendship we might have. I'd lost a hell of a lot of people over the years due to my power. I'd made a lot of mistakes.

I didn't want to make that same mistake again. My life had began anew after joining this Court. Time to be better than the lonely fae I once was. Time to belong to something more than just myself.

Sucking a deep breath in through my nose, I stared at Tiarnan but I didn't reach my mind toward him. Balor had given me an order, but he hadn't given me a command, which meant the full extent of his power wasn't behind his words.

Even then, it was hard to push against what he wanted me to do, but I managed.

The hardest part now would be lying to him.

"He's telling the truth," I finally said, ripping my gaze away from Tiarnan's face. "But I'm sure you already knew that. He's a Fianna. His honour is the most important thing to him. He wouldn't go to his Prince for help if he wasn't sincere."

Okay, so maybe I'd laid it on a little thick, but I didn't know how Balor would react if he knew I'd lied to him. After the little scene at the bar, I didn't want to find out. He'd reminded me just how dangerous he could be.

"Fine," Balor said in a clipped tone. "You can stay for now. I'll have someone find you a room. In the meantime..." He gestured at the curving staircase and sent Tiarnan a smile full of sharp teeth. "Make yourself at home."

∼

*A*fter Balor strode away, Moira and Elise both gave me a strange look before scurrying off down the corridor. It was just me and Tiarnan now, and a super uncomfortable silence that made me wish I'd followed after my friends. The traitors.

Tiarnan cleared his throat. "Thanks for not reading my mind, though I hope you know what you're doing. If Balor finds out—"

"He won't find out," I said. "I'm surprised you could tell I didn't."

"You've done it to me a few times before, remember? Your expression was different now, and I didn't feel your power like I have in the past. It kind of...radiates off of you. It's quite impressive."

"Thanks?" I blew out a hot breath. "Just don't tell anyone, okay?"

"I won't." A beat passed. "Why didn't you, by the way? I thought that was your job as a member of the guard team."

"It is my job. But I don't like using it in certain situations. Like this one. You're my...friend, I guess. I've made the mistake of listening to my friends' thoughts in the past, and I know how that ends up. With everyone angry. Most of the time, said friends never spoke to me again."

"I can imagine," he said quietly. "Though it was still a risk. I would have understood if you'd done it."

"No, you wouldn't have." I gave him a sad smile. "But anyway, all that is over. And Balor won't find out, so I won't have to face his wrath like those poor humans did."

Tiarnan cocked his head, eyebrows furrowing. "What are you talking about? What wrath?"

I'd forgotten that he'd been out of the loop. News probably hadn't yet reached Ireland, and even then, Fionn wouldn't have confided in him. So, I filled Tiarnan in on the past twenty-four hours. The Sluaghs, the cemetery, and the supes we'd found down in the cellar. And the bit about Balor's eye flames, too.

Tiarnan looked troubled when I'd finished the story. He glanced behind him, clearly searching to see if our Prince was heading our way with an update about his room situation. "Sometimes, I do not understand Balor's actions. Burning down a human establishment when humans were still in it? Not very honourable."

"Yeah, I didn't think so either."

"And to do so as a way to set free vampires and shifters." Tiarnan's eyes went dark. "Unacceptable."

"Hey." I frowned at him. "You're talking to a half-shifter here. I know Fionn is against the whole vamp alliance thing, but that kind of talk isn't going to win you many friends in this House."

"Right. Of course. Sorry." His eyes cleared, the light coming back. "I didn't mean you, of course. You're different. You're—"

"I'm not different. I am a half-shifter," I repeated. "Don't forget it again."

Footsteps echoed on the marble floor, saving me from the strange new tension that peppered the air. There was a lot I liked about Tiarnan. He was about ninety-nine percent perfect as far as I could tell. But there was just that one percent that was kind of hard to ignore. He hated other supernaturals, just like Fionn. Oh, and he wasn't Balor Beimnech.

That was both a pro and a con as far as I was concerned.

I turned toward the footsteps, fully expecting to lay my eyes on said Prince, but instead, it was Kyle. He scurried about, a clipboard clutched tight to his chest. He scanned the lobby, and his tight expression relaxed when he saw me.

"There you are. I've been searching for that vampire Sluagh info you asked me about. I got a hit, and you're going to want to see this."

10

*E*veryone clustered around Kyle's desk, including Tiarnan. We were all there. The whole team had filed into the command station to see what Kyle had found.

Being in the same room with them at the same damn time—Tiarnan and Balor—was...interesting. I could feel both of them near me, could sense their eyes shooting quick glances my way, though I didn't know if I was just making that up.

I was probably making it up.

"So, see here," Kyle said, cutting through my jumbled thoughts about the two fae males in my life. "I found a manuscript about a vampire who was turned into a Sluagh. Way back in the 1300s. There's not much information here about how this happened, who did it, or what happened to her next."

Balor leaned forward and braced his hands on the desk. "So, this is something that has happened before. Did you get any more hits? Any information that could possibly help us find out who is doing this and how to stop him?"

"Well, not exactly..." Kyle tapped a few keys. "But I did find something kind of curious that I thought might be of interest."

A photograph flashed up before us. It was fairly recent and showed a female vampire whose eyes were a deep crimson red lined with black. Her long, scraggly hair hung down to her waist, and her lips were stained with red.

"This is a female vampire who came up in my search. See, the name of the vampire in the book was pretty unique, which was why I decided to do a quick Google search. Just to see if anything turned up. I was kind of surprised that anything did, to be totally honest. The original vamp was turned hundreds of years ago. She should be nothing more than dust by now, so this is probably a coincidence and—"

"Enough," Balor said. "Short version, Kyle. Who is this vampire?"

Kyle tapped a few more keys to bring up the scan of the manuscript. He pointed at the screen, tapping his finger next to a few words that looked kind of like gibberish to me. Old English, probably. "They mention her name here, the one who was turned. Alyxianne Millandresum. Weird name, right?"

The photo flashed up on the screen again. "This female here? Same name. What are the odds? It's one of the most bizarre names I've ever seen, and I've spent a lot of time combing through records, so that's saying something."

Tiarnan let out a low whistle. "How could she be

alive after all this time if she's been transformed into a Sluagh?"

"I don't know, but I found an address for her. So, you could just go and ask her about it."

"Where is she?" Balor asked in a low growl.

"She's in Shoreditch," Kyle said. "And it sounds like she runs a shop called The Skull Cauldron."

～

The guards all convened in the sparring room. It was time for Balor to choose his team for the mission, something he liked to do at the start of every new lead. I assumed he'd want Cormac or Duncan to go with him on this one, maybe Moira. It would likely involve some fighting, and they were the strong ones when it came to that.

"Because of the attack on our House yesterday, along with the news that has broken in the human press, I would like my strongest guards to stay at the House this evening." Balor scanned the group, and then his eye landed on me. "Clark, I would like you to go interrogate the vampire."

"Um...seriously?"

"You have proven yourself time and again," he said. "You held your own in the cemetery. Besides, if the vampire refuses to talk, you can get some much needed information that the others cannot."

That old chestnut.

Sometimes, I really hated my power.

"I'll go with her," Tiarnan quickly said. "You obviously don't intend for her to go alone. This could be my chance to prove some worth to this House, in exchange for you taking me in when I have no home."

I frowned. While it was honourable of Tiarnan to volunteer for this wild-ass mission, and while his warrior skills would no doubt come in handy, I had assumed that Balor would join me. We'd gone to check out the bar together. If I was going to interrogate this vampire, he should be the one to go with me.

"Maybe it's best not to introduce someone new to this particular case at this point in time..." I trailed off and glanced at Balor, but he strategically avoided my eyes. "Maybe those of us who started the case should finish the case."

A.K.A. you should go with me, Balor.

Balor's jaw rippled. "You're right, Clark. We need fae on the case who have knowledge and experience of what we've already learned. That's part of the reason I'm sending you."

My lips began to turn up in the corners.

"But I have a lot on my agenda for the day. Tiarnan is a strong fighter. You two will make a good team." He spoke the words with about as much emotion as a tortoise.

Out of the corner of my eye, I could feel Moira and Elise both glance at me. I'd told them everything that had happened between me and Balor, and they knew how I felt. I couldn't bear to look at them now, not when he was back to pushing me away as hard as he could.

One step forward, two steps back.

"Fine," I said in a clipped tone. "Tiarnan and I will go talk to the vamp."

We waited until half an hour before closing time. It was the best way to ensure that the vampire would still be banging around in the shop while *hopefully* avoiding a scene in front of dozens of humans. There might still be a few trailing through the shelves, but the daytime crowds should be cleared out by then.

The shop was located deep within hipster territory, the land of kombucha, thick-rimmed glasses, and beards. The sun had already begun to set behind the city skyline, such was the February light, and the headlights of cars swept across us as we strode down the pavement.

We were both carrying swords, but we'd hidden them beneath long coats for once. With the growing concern about supernaturals, we thought it best to stay as incognito as possible.

"You ready for this?" Tiarnan asked, his eyes alert, his shoulders tense. We continued down the street, passing underneath the glow of streetlamps.

"Not really," I said dryly. "You? Did you do these kinds of missions for Fionn when you were at his House?"

"I can't say I've ever had the pleasure of tracking down a vampire Sluagh, no. But I have done *other* missions. Fighting off invading werewolf packs. Tracking down vampires who were killing entire villages. That kind of thing."

I frowned. "They don't do that anymore, Tiarnan. It's been decades since other supes gave in to the violent side of their nature."

"*At the moment*, they don't do any of that. But it's only a matter of time. Nature is nature, and there is no fighting it off forever."

I stopped short on the pavement and turned toward him. Humans streamed past us, barely even giving us a moment's notice. "Look, you and I get along, and I'm glad you came back to London when Fionn wouldn't let you into your House. But if we're going to work together on this case, things will go a lot more smoothly if you don't talk about others supes like they're the scum of the earth."

For a moment, Tiarnan looked at me. He seemed surprised by my outburst. To be honest, I was kind of surprised by myself, too. I'd spent years doing investigative work for supes, but I'd never been particularly fond of any vamps or shifters that I'd met. They tended to punch holes in my walls, after all. But that didn't mean I thought they deserved scorn, or worse. I was pretty sure that Tiarnan would happily fight a vampire to the death, if given the opportunity. That wasn't right. And I didn't have to accept it.

Finally, Tiarnan's expression softened. "Alright. If it means that much to you, then I won't bring it up again."

"Good."

"Good." He smiled. "And I'll try to understand things from your perspective."

That was more than I'd asked for, and I appreciated that he'd even offered to try. If Balor and I had been in this situation, he never would have caved. He would have said whatever he damn well wanted to say, and he never would have tried to see things my way.

Point in the Tiarnan column. Maybe he'd learn that not all supes were bad.

"You know what? Thanks." I shot Tiarnan a smile. "I'll have to admit I didn't expect you to respond this way. The people I've always known have never been so reasonable."

Tiarnan motioned for us to continue down the street. "The people you've known from your past? You've never really said much about that before."

I stiffened. "No, and there's reason for that. It's not a fun story to tell."

"I'm a good listener. If you ever want someone to talk to...well, I'm all ears."

I flicked my eyes his way, considering him. Obviously, I wasn't going to tell him a damn thing about my past. Not concrete details anyway. But that didn't mean I was immune to the temptation of it. I'd kept the truth wrapped up so tight in my mind for all these years that I didn't even allow myself to think of it. Partly out of self-defence. What if I stumbled onto another mind reader? But also partly because I couldn't bear to face it, even in my own mind.

"Maybe some other time," I said quietly.

"On a date, perhaps?"

My neck flushed with heat. "You're seriously asking me out on a date two seconds after you insulted shifters? Even knowing that my father was one?"

"Ah, there's a little nugget of information. Your father was the shifter. Not your mother. What kind of shifter was he then? What do you transform into?"

I pressed my lips firmly together. I did not want to talk about my father.

"I don't know. I've never actually shifted."

Tiarnan arched a brow. "But your father—"

"I said I don't know."

Tiarnan fell silent for a moment, and the clanging of the city rose up around us. Cabbies honked, wind rustled through the buildings, and the buzz of human voices drifted down the street. The sound soothed my raw nerves. It was the pulse of the city, a living, breathing thing that made my charged heart feel calm.

Tiarnan cleared his throat. "Listen, I know I might be way out of line here, so you can tell me to bugger off if I am. I know a shifter here in London. A good lad. I can talk to him for you, see if he'd be available to talk you through the shift. He's done it for others."

"I thought you hated shifters," I said in a flat voice.

"I never said that," he replied. "I can't ignore how dangerous many of them can be, due to their animalistic instincts. That doesn't mean I distrust all of them. You're a perfect example of the good that some can do."

"What makes you think I even want to know how to shift?"

He lifted a shoulder in a shrug. "Just a hunch."

"Well, your hunch is wrong. The reason I've never shifted is because I've never tried."

"Haven't tried because you didn't want to do it or because you didn't know where to start?"

"Tiarnan. This might be the time when I tell you to bugger off."

"Alright." He held up his hands and laughed. "I won't push it. Just remember the offer is there if you decide you want to take me up on it."

"Hmph."

Truth was, I was a little intrigued. I knew next to

nothing about the process of shifting, and sometimes I wished I could open myself up to that part of me. But I was scared. What would happen when I shifted? Would I lose control? Would I know how to shift back? And what kind of animal would I become?

And the scariest thought: what if I turned into something horribly dangerous? Something that wanted to kill. Werewolves were infamous for finding it difficult to control themselves. There were even were-lions and were-bears. That kind of animal shouldn't be set loose on London.

On my own, I had nothing and no one to stop me if I transformed into a dangerous beast. So, I'd never wanted to try.

But that was way too personal to explain to Tiarnan. I couldn't imagine he'd understand anyway.

"Ah, here we are." I slowed to a stop outside of The Skull Cauldron. We peered in through the window. On display were a wide variety of painted skulls, each turned upside down to hold...well, I wasn't sure exactly. Did people actually drink out of these things?

"Looks like it's still open." Tiarnan slipped his hand beneath his coat, rested his palm on his sword. "Reckon we should go inside."

11

A little bell dinged when I pushed on the door of the shop. As we stepped inside, the temperature warmed considerably, and the scent of pachouli flooded my nose. A strange prickle of magic coursed along my skin, a sensation I only got when near considerable power.

Probably not a fantastic sign in this particular situation.

I turned my gaze toward Tiarnan. He was scanning the shop with keen eyes, his coat now dropping away to reveal the hilt of his golden sword. He looked strong and powerful, like the warrior he was. Like he'd been in far more dangerous battles than this one.

Not that this was a battle. This was a sneaky excursion into one of the weirdest shops I'd had the pleasure of browsing. I mean, who made cauldrons out of skulls? Sluagh vampires apparently.

"Do you feel that?" I asked as quietly as I could. The shop might be open, but there was no one in it.

Not a single customer drifted through the crammed rows of cauldron skulls. There were probably at least two hundred of the things. Each one was painted differently with unique shapes, colour combinations, and markings. I hoped they weren't real, but...I wasn't entirely sure they weren't.

The spot between Tiarnan's eyes creased when he frowned. "Feel what?"

"The magic. Like a shimmer almost, only a lot creepier." I nibbled on my bottom lip before continuing. "I think the most accurate description would be that it feels like someone is holding a chunk of long hair and they are sliding the strands all over my skin."

"Yeah, I can see where you came up with the creepy comment," Tiarnan said with a shudder. "But no. I don't feel anything of the sort."

Weird.

I began to drift down one row of skull cauldrons, glancing around for any information that might come in handy. Some kind of, I don't know, book or something that spelled out all the answers. Or a photo album showing the vampire and the sorcerer standing together with their arms thrown around each other's necks, grinning from ear to ear. That would be useful in tracking down the culprit.

But no such luck. There wasn't even a neon sign flashing the name of the sorcerer.

"Where do you think she is, anyway?" I stopped in front of a skull that was painted in stripes of varying shades of red. It looked a lot like the skulls on Balor's throne. Glancing around, I took the skull and slid it into the pocket of my coat. "Who opens a shop and then just doesn't stick around to man the cash register?"

"I imagine she doesn't get a lot of customers."

The door dinged, and we both whirled toward it, our stances nearly identical. Shoulders thrown back, eyes narrowed, hands on sword hilts, just in case the vampire Sluagh decided to attack.

Unfortunately (or fortunately, depending on how you looked at it), the new arrivals at the scene were not of the vampire Sluagh variety. Instead, two human girls, probably university-aged, threw open the door, both giggling madly as they stumbled inside.

I let go of my hilt, and the coat drifted shut around it just in time. They stopped suddenly when they spotted me staring at them. I cleared my throat and glanced away, pretending to examine a green-horned skull. They continued their hushed conversation, tripping through the aisles with about as much grace as a steam engine.

"It will be the funniest thing," one of them hissed to the other. "How many should we take?"

"The whole lot if we can manage," the other girl giggled back. "Imagine the looks on their faces when they wake up to the story."

"Crazed fae serial killer takes down hundreds, paints the skulls, and leaves them out as a warning for anyone who tries to stop them!"

I dropped my hand away from the horned skull, and heard Tiarnan's whispered warning a second too late. Eyes narrowed, I stalked toward the girls. "Excuse me, what the fuck do you think you're talking about?"

The smiles died; their eyes flicked across me and then toward Tiarnan. They both shifted on their feet, seemingly realising that they'd made a humongous mistake.

"Erm," the darker-haired one said. "We were just taking the piss. Didn't mean anything by it. We'll be going now."

"No, we won't," the redhead said, narrowing her eyes and crossing her arms over her chest. "You're one of them, aren't ya? The fae. A supernatural terrorist. What have you got under your coat? Something tells me it's not a woolly jumper."

"Lucy, come on," the brunette replied, tugging on her friend's arm. "This ain't worth it."

"Of course it's worth it. We've been talking about how awful the fae are and what we'd do if we ever found one. Well, we've got two here in front of us now. Call the coppers. Tell 'em they were trying to steal the skulls for some kind of voodoo magic."

"How clever of you." I smiled and pointed at the far corner of the shop. "You might notice this place has CCTV, so you're all out of luck on framing us this time."

"No matter. Fire destroys cameras, right? You should know, since your kind are so fond of burning down our buildings. Some say it was even your Prince, and we intend to find out. Imagine what will happen when the world finds out. No more bowing down before you lot. We'll get our city back, and get rid of you."

My bond with Balor snapped tight, and a deep, dark rage began to kindle inside of me.

"You better go now," I said in a low growl that sounded so much like my Master's that it made a warning bell clang inside of me. But I couldn't stop the rage, even if I wanted. "Before I do something I'll live to regret."

Lucy's friend swallowed hard. "Come on, Lucy. She looks like she means it, and I'm pretty sure they have weapons. We can get them on something else some other time."

Lucy glared at me for one second more before she spun on her heels and stomped out of the store. The door slammed shut behind them, and all the breath whooshed from my lungs. Hands shaking, I grasped onto the nearest shelf and clung on tight. My adrenaline had been on a rampage, charging through me like a tornado. Now that the moment was over, I felt weak, like all the fight had suddenly gone out of me.

What the hell was that, Clark?

"You alright?" Tiarnan strode over to the door and twisted the lock. We probably should have done that the second we'd come inside.

"I am feeling a little shaky, to be honest. For several reasons. I'm also pretty sure I only made things worse. Whatever they were planning, they'll keep on planning it. And maybe a worse version of it."

Tiarnan gave a solemn nod. "It sounded like they wanted to frame Balor for a bunch of murders, and the Court as a whole."

"It seems like everyone wants to frame Balor," I muttered.

Drifting away from the door, Tiarnan ran a finger along the wooden surface of the nearest shelf. He lifted his finger, inspected it, and then blew some dust into the air. "He's a good target."

"A *good* target?" I crossed my arms.

"Wrong choice of words," Tiarnan said smoothly.

"He's the *right* target if you want to make a point. Nemain wanted Lesley to set him up, so that she could destroy the fae alliances with the vamps and the shifters. These humans want to take him down because they're scared. Take down the leader, take down the Court. They want their city back. They want London to be free of supes."

"We're going to have to put a stop to that. As much as I understand their fear, this city is ours, too."

"Yes. You're right." Tiarnan frowned around at the shop. "There's a thin layer of dust on everything."

"Like you said, she probably doesn't get many customers." I rubbed the top of the nearest cauldron, and a streak of dust clung to my skin. "And I don't suppose that Sluaghs are particularly skilled in the cleaning department."

Tiarnan quickly moved around the back of the counter where an old cash register sat proudly on display. The counter was empty other than the register and a flyer that advertised the opening of a new play called 'It's Skulls in Your Head'. Shoreditch really was an odd neighbourhood sometimes.

My heartbeat picked up speed as Tiarnan leaned down and poked at the drawers. "Erm, like I said, this place has CCTV, and the vamp could be back at any moment."

"Yes," Tiarnan said softly. "It has CCTV, but I don't think the vampire is going to be back anytime soon. I actually don't think she's been here in at least a few days. Maybe even a week."

Tiarnan pulled a contraption from beneath the counter. It was a tall, thin metal rod that poked through at least a hundred tiny pieces of paper.

Receipts. He pulled the top one off the pile and waved it toward me.

When I clutched the receipt in my hand, I read the contents quickly. It was the sale of one skull cauldron for a ridiculously expensive price of two hundred and twenty five pounds. Furrowing my brow, I looked back up at Tiarnan.

"I don't understand."

"Look at the date."

And so I did. "A week ago. That doesn't mean anything. I can't imagine someone buys a skull cauldron every day. They cost over two hundred quid, for fuck's sake."

"The dust, the receipt, the unmanned shop." Tiarnan lifted his shoulders in a shrug. "It all adds up to one missing vampire Sluagh."

Sighing, I closed my eyes and sank against the countertop for support. "Great. So, this was just another dead end then. We're no closer to finding out what the sorcerer is up to or even who he is."

"We do have one bit of information we didn't have before."

I lifted a brow in question.

"The sorcerer must have found out about this original vampire Sluagh and came here for her."

"That is a legitimate concern." I loosed a breath. "But if that's the case, then could we have some sort of mole inside the Court again? Like with Lesley?"

"I doubt there would be two fae inside of Balor's Court who would be willing to go up against him." Tiarnan pushed the receipt back on top of the pile. "Besides, it looks like the vampire went missing before we even found out about this place. I doubt it's connected."

I pointed at a door just behind Tiarnan's shoulder. "While we're here, should we take a look? There might be something interesting back there. Might not lead us to the sorcerer but it could potentially give us some background info on the vamp."

Tiarnan glanced over his shoulder, and then flicked off the lights, just in case anyone passed the windows out front. "Okay, let's give it a look."

We tried the knob, and it wasn't locked. Another sign that the vampire's departure probably wasn't voluntary. If she'd gone somewhere, she would have locked things up to keep the shop safe. Luckily for her, no one really wanted to trek inside a shop full of skulls to steal something. Except humans who wanted to frame our Prince, apparently.

The door creaked on its hinges, which was nice and ominous. Exactly what I wanted to hear as we were breaking into the stock room of a vampire Sluagh.

Inside, we found more of a bedroom than a storage area. There was a tiny cot pushed up against the far wall, covered in a mattress but no sheets. A small table sat next to it, holding a small lamp, a box of cigarettes, and an empty beer bottle. In the opposite corner, there was a refrigerator. I didn't need to open it to know what was inside. Blood bags. Probably a lot of them.

Other than that, the room was empty.

"This was incredibly unhelpful," I said, turning toward the door. As I did, something in the shadowy corner caught my eye. A dark form on the floor.

Sucking in a sharp breath, I reached for the hilt of my sword but stopped when the form became clearer, my eyes adjusting to the low light of the room.

"Tiarnan, look," I said, heart beating hard in my chest. "I think we may have found the vampire."

Because the form was not a body at all. It was a massive pile of ash.

12

When we returned to Court, we filled Balor and the team in on what we had found, which wasn't much in the grand scheme of things. A pile of ash did not equal answers. All it equalled was a dead vampire, one who had likely died from a result of the Sluagh curse. She'd lasted a hell of a long time, which was curious enough on its own. But to die now? With everything going on? Tiarnan was probably onto something. The sorcerer had probably tracked her down.

Speaking of Tiarnan...

He gently grabbed my elbow as I headed into the back room to practice my fighting skills. For now, we had no leads, and we had no next move until Kyle could scrounge up some more information about our elusive sorcerer. In the meantime, I figured I would train. It was going to take a long time for me to master the sword. I had a long way to go, and I wanted to spend as many hours as I could on honing my skills.

"There's something I wanted to ask you," he said

quietly as Balor stalked up behind us. Balor's eye flashed as he took in Tiarnan's hand on my arm, the warrior stance, the strong yet boyish smile. Balor's expression was close to blank, but I swore I could hear a low rumble coming from his throat.

"Am I interrupting something?" Balor asked in a crisp tone.

"I just wanted to speak to Clark about something."

Balor crossed his arms over his chest. "Go on then. Whatever you have to say to one of my guards, you can say to me, too."

Tiarnan shifted on his feet. "Balor, listen, I don't know if that's such a good—"

"You should say it in front of me."

Power washed over my skin, a magic so deep and dark that it made me gasp out loud. It pulsed along my body, tendrils of it snaking around my arms, my legs, my neck. I wanted to curl up inside of it, to give in to every desire that churned deep within my gut. I shuddered.

And then the sensation fell away.

Damn Balor Beimnech. That wasn't fair, and he knew it.

I glanced up at Tiarnan. His eyebrows were pinched. Had he felt that same energy? Had that same magic pulled at his skin? Probably not. I had a feeling that had been meant for me and me alone.

And I'd responded exactly the way Balor had wanted.

"Fine," Tiarnan said through gritted teeth before turning toward me. "Clark, I wanted to ask if you'd like to join me for dinner tonight. I haven't had the opportunity to dine in the restaurant here since it opened, and I was hoping we could make it a date."

Oh my god. Tiarnan hadn't just asked me out on a date in front of Balor. Had he? No, that was impossible. Cheeks flaming, I gritted my teeth and shifted my eyes toward Balor. I fully expected him to lift that eye patch of his and burn a hole right through the middle of the Court.

There was no way in hell he was going to let this one fly. Tiarnan was toast, and I had no idea how I was going to stop the fiery temper coming his way.

But Balor was...strangely calm. His stance remained strong and sure, but he didn't lift his chest in some macho display of power. He didn't force his magic over my skin. And he didn't touch the damn eye patch. Instead, he gave us a smile. Or a strange, unsettling close proximity to one.

"Clark, you aren't going to keep this nice warrior waiting for an answer, now are you?"

My heart thumped hard in my chest. What was he doing? He kept pushing me away, sure. And I was still irritated with him about the burning building, yes. But surely, he didn't want me to *actually* go on a date with another male? I mean, there was something there between us, right? I hadn't imagined it all in my head.

For the first time in days, I turned my power toward a member of my own Court. Well, Balor didn't really count as a member, did he? I closed my eyes and focused, letting my mind reach out toward his. I wanted to know what he was really thinking. No, I *needed* to know. I was tired of playing this game with him, the one I always lost without fail.

Instead of bumping up against his ever-present

mental wall, I found my mind welcomed in, just as it had been in the abandoned tube station.

I don't like it when you try to read my mind, Clark.

Well, maybe if you weren't so exasperatingly annoying, I wouldn't do it.

I don't understand why you're annoyed. A pause. *I know you're fond of Tiarnan. He is a kind fae. He would make a good mate. You should accept his offer.*

Are you serious?

There wasn't a hint of jealousy in his voice nor was there any emotion at all. Balor was being his Princely self, the one who couldn't care less about those around him. Maybe I'd been wrong all this time. Maybe he didn't feel anything toward me. Or, if he had, it was gone now. He didn't rage because he wasn't even the slightest bit angry.

Maybe he really didn't care if I went on a date with Tiarnan.

Hell, it was Saturday night. He probably planned on going to his club. There, he would find a brunette to shag his bloody heart out.

I didn't want to be with someone like that. So cold and calculating. So distant. So unable to form an actual connection with anyone. I needed someone open and honest. Someone honourable and caring. I needed someone like Tiarnan.

Fine.

I snapped my mind out of his head and back into mine, and then I opened my eyes. Tiarnan was frowning at us both, and it looked as though we'd attracted a bit of a crowd. All of the guard team was standing in the background, watching. Elise was mimicking popcorn munching while Kyle literally had a bag of crisps in his hands.

"Perhaps I should go," Tiarnan said slowly. "I can see my question has caused some tension that I did not intend."

"No, don't go." I placed a soft hand on his arm and smiled wide when Balor's gaze followed my movement. "We were just having a little chat. I'd love to go on a date with you. What time?"

~

This time, Balor did not have a dress sent to my room, not that I was surprised. He was probably long gone, out pulling girls at his club. Moira and Elise swung by to help, along with Ondine, bringing with them snacks of the wine and chocolate variety.

"Here. Reinforcements." Moira plopped the drink in my lap while Elise began to fuss with my hair. "Thought you might need it."

I frowned down at the bottle, wincing when Elise pulled just a little too tight. "I'm not sure you're supposed to get drunk *before* the date."

"Not drunk. Just a glass. It'll take the edge off and make you less nervous. I'm always so on edge before a date. How are you feeling?" Ondine asked, brushing her dark hair out of her face. Since the attack, Ondine had kept to herself more than she had before. I rarely saw her now. I was so busy with the guard team, and she was so busy helping out with the gardening duties around the Court.

"I'm okay, actually," I said, but I accepted a wine

glass anyway. "I mean, it's not like I don't know the guy. Maybe I'd be more nervous if I'd found him on Tinder or something."

Ondine clinked her glass against mine, and we all drank. Despite my hesitation, I actually was looking forward to the date. I hadn't yet checked out the five-star restaurant, and Tiarnan was a nice, handsome fae. But I didn't want it to feel like it was this grand event that required hours of preparation. Still, they all insisted I look my very best, which involved a lot of primping, a lot of preening, and a hell of a lot of shoving my way into a too-tight dress.

I tugged on the clingy gold material and slid my feet into a pair of heels. Ondine had loaned me both the dress and the shoes, being the closest in size. She was taller than me by a couple of inches, but that worked out just fine for me. It meant my arse wasn't hanging out the back of this bloody dress.

"I don't know, girls. This seems a smidge over the top."

"You look great." Ondine clapped her hands and grinned. "Now, spin. Let's take it all in."

With a sigh, I whirled. I didn't feel any better about the outfit after the spin than I had before, but they sure seemed happy about it.

"Right." Elise opened the door, and Moira practically pushed me out into the corridor. "Have fun!"

~

I waddled my way into the restaurant. When Balor had renovated the old Battersea Power Station into a home for the Crimson Court, he'd added a five-star restaurant to the ground floor. Fae streamed by me in ordinary clothes—jeans, jumpers, flats. Several cast me a side-eye, but I did my best not to pay them any mind.

Instead, I was transfixed by what I saw before me. The lofted ceilings of the power station were present even here. The walls had been painted a smooth crimson, rising high to meet the domed ceiling above. This was the only floor in this wing of the building, so the skylights revealed the glow of the city beyond. Chandeliers hung in regular intervals, highlighting the quiet booths that lined each wall. Everything was golden and red and elaborate, even the tall, golden podium that stood before me.

A fae, one whom I'd yet to meet, flicked his eyes up and down my dress, but didn't say a word. He had short-cropped purple hair, but his unique, vibrant colouring did not match his lifted nose and stiff shoulders. He tapped his pen against his notepad.

"Hi, I'm hear to meet—"

"Tiarnan, Fianna of House Futrail. Yes, I know. He is waiting in the back booth. I shall escort you to your seat."

Well, this guy was certainly formal. He was even wearing a tux that looked like it had been ironed about a thousand times. It couldn't possibly get any stiffer than it was. A bow tie was cinched tight around his large neck, and dark stubble lined his jaw.

He flicked his fingers and twisted sharply on his heels, striding toward the back corner of the room with such precision that he looked like he was in the middle of some kind of tap dance routine.

I followed just behind him, teetering a bit in my

heels. The girls had only been trying to help, hoping that the added height would give off some sort of enhanced sex appeal. I was pretty sure it was doing the total opposite.

Mr. Clicky Heels came to a sudden stop at a table. Tiarnan's profile shifted into view from beyond the crimson booth. His eyes opened wide; his mouth even parted. He wore a casual suit that fit him well, highlighting the thick biceps, the muscular chest. He stood slowly, giving me an appreciative smile.

"Wow, Clark. You look incredible." He hurried over to the back of my chair but realised a second too late that he couldn't very well pull a booth out from under a table. "Ah, well. Nevermind then. You've distracted me to the point that I couldn't remember the difference between a chair and a booth."

My cheeks flushed with heat. "Thanks. You're looking very nice yourself."

He smiled, dimples dotting his cheeks. Had he had them before? I'd never noticed until now.

"I took the liberty of ordering for the both of us. The wine is on its way now."

"Oh." I gave him a slight smile. "Okay then. I guess that's fine."

"Good."

The server arrived with the bottle of wine. It was decanted into the glasses, poured with just as much precision as I'd received from the greeter at the podium. Once he'd left us to our own devices, Tiarnan and I just kind of stared at each other.

"So, tell me," he said after clearing his throat. "How is Court life treating you? Are you settling in alright? I know you've only been here, what, a couple of weeks?"

That was a difficult one to answer. Until a week ago, I'd planned on getting the hell out of dodge as fast as I possibly could. I'd only just decided to stay, and I had no idea how long I would actually be able to call this place my home. That said, Tiarnan didn't need to know all that. It would only lead to more questions.

"It's actually been easier than I thought it would be," I said. "At first, I was a little bit skeptical, I won't lie. I've been on my own my entire life. This is a totally different kind of life, you know? But everyone has been super welcoming. I've even made some friends."

"Cheers to that." He smiled as we clinked our glasses together. "And what's Balor like? Different than what you expected? Better? Worse?"

"Ah." My heart felt a little funny at the mention of our Prince's name. "I think I'd rather not talk about Balor."

As if summoned, the very Prince who had told me to come on this date appeared in the door of the restaurant. His gaze flicked from booth to booth. I curled my hands tight around the cloth napkin in my lap. The material was smooth against my skin, but that didn't stop my nails from bending against the force of my grip. His gaze landed on me, a strange expression flickered across his face, and then he was gone.

13

My heart raced, and I swallowed down a lump in my throat. What the hell had that been all about? Why had Balor come here, looking like he wanted to tear the chandeliers from the ceiling? He had nothing to be angry about. He'd told me to come here. Not only out loud but also in his mind.

He had made it more than clear that this was what he wanted me to do.

"Is something wrong?" Tiarnan frowned, twisted in his seat to stare at the doorway. He wouldn't find anything. Balor was gone.

"Nothing," I said quickly. "I just thought I saw...nothing. What were we talking about?"

"Balor. And I have a feeling he has something to do with that look on your face. You only ever look that way when he's around." Tiarnan's voice was even, conversational, and completely free of accusation. But still, his words made me feel defensive, like I'd been up to something wrong.

"Like I said, I'd rather not talk about Balor on our date. Maybe you could tell me about one of your missions as a Fianna."

"Okay," he said, nodding slowly. "I'll agree to not mention Balor again if you'll answer one question for me."

My heart thumped hard. One question. It could be anything. It could be about my past. It could be about my parents. He could want to know what had happened all those years ago when so many lives had been lost.

Shit, Clark. Get yourself together. Don't even think those kinds of thoughts.

"One question," I said in a cracked voice. "But I have the right to change my mind if I don't want to answer whatever it is that you want to know."

He chuckled. "You know, for someone who can read minds, you're extremely secretive."

I lifted a brow. "I've never pretended to be otherwise. What's the question?"

His expression sobered immediately. "What was going on between you and Balor earlier, back in the command station? You two went into a very strange trance-like state, almost as though he was reading your mind and you were reading his."

My shoulders relaxed.

"Okay, I can answer that. Since joining the Court, I've begun to have the ability to have two-way conversations with a few select fae. Masters, in particular. I've only been able to do it with Fionn and Balor so far. Of course, that could change."

"You were having a two-way mind conversation

with Balor?" Tiarnan lifted his brow. "What were you talking about?"

"Ah, ah." I held up a finger and wagged it back and forth. "We agreed to one question. Now, I've answered it. It's *my* turn to ask *you* something."

"Alright, alright." He held up his hands in defeat and grinned. "What deep, dark secrets of mine do you want to know?"

I leaned forward, conspiratorially. "What's your favourite Taylor Swift song?"

His eyes opened in surprise, and then he laughed. "My favourite—? You've got to be taking the piss, right?"

"I'm afraid not." I crossed my arms over my chest and gave him a stern look. "Now, I've answered your question. It's your turn, and I won't let you weasel your way out of this one. This is serious business, don't you know."

"Fine. You've got me. I have listened to a song or two of hers. My favourite would have to be *Shake It Off.*"

"Such an obvious answer."

Tiarnan took a sip of his wine and winked at me over the glass. "I assume you have a better answer. Go on then. Educate me on all things pop. Or is it country?"

The smile died on my lips when I saw a shadowy figure lurking by the doorway of the restaurant. It disappeared from view just as quickly as it had appeared. A moment later, it whisked by once again. It was large, tall, and very Princely in the way it held itself. I didn't even have to see him to know that it was Balor.

"Excuse me." I dropped the napkin on the table and stood. "I'll be right back."

"Clark, wait," Tiarnan called after me as I strode, fists clenched, toward the shadow. "What's going on?"

But Tiarnan would have to wait. I had another pesky male to deal with.

I stomped past the gold podium, away from the clusters of expensive chandeliers, and out into the marble hallway. As I'd expected, Balor was there, pacing back and forth like an expectant father in a hospital waiting room.

Fisting my hands, I propped them on my dress-clad hips and glared at him. "Are you actually spying on my date with Tiarnan?"

He slowed to a stop, clenched his jaw. "If I were spying on your date, I would be in there instead of out here."

"I saw you come inside." I strode up to him and poked a finger in his chest. Once, twice, three times. And then a fourth time for good measure. "What. Are. You. Doing. Here?"

He grabbed my wrist in his hand to stop the poking. "Having fun? Enjoying your glass of wine?"

"What's it to you? You're the one who told me I should come on this date in the first place. I gave you plenty of time to object."

"Why would I object? We aren't in a relationship. We aren't even in the early beginnings of one."

"No, we aren't. Did you have fun at your club tonight? How many brunettes did you manage to shag?"

He scowled. "This is ridiculous. Why did you even

come out here? You're supposed to be in the restaurant enjoying a meal with *him*."

"Because I saw you lurking around out here. It was creeping me out."

"Interesting how easily you were distracted from your date."

I threw up my hands. "Whatever, Balor. I've had enough of this. I'm going back inside. Continue to creep around here all you want, but I'm not coming out again, not until dinner is over. And then...well, and then who knows where we'll go next. I do have a bottle of wine in my room."

Balor let out a low growl. "Good. Return to your date. You shouldn't even be out here."

Oh, he was just so annoying! A part of me seriously wanted to stand out here yelling at him all evening long, but Tiarnan was waiting. He'd clearly seen me walk out the front door, and he was probably wondering when—or if—I was coming back. Balor might be maddening, but I couldn't let him suck me into his orbit. He was like a meteor. A fiery one. And he destroyed everything in his path.

"Have a nice night. Maybe you should go do something useful." I spun on my heels and stomped back into the restaurant. Well, stomp was a generous way to describe the way I lurched around in the heels. As I approached the booth, I smoothed the hair away from my face and tried to calm my breathing. Balor's arrival had made my heart race. Because of the whole anger thing. Sometimes, the Prince really made me want to scream.

When I turned the corner, I pasted on a smile, trying to come up with a reasonable explanation that

Tiarnan might understand. I had a feeling he wasn't going to buy it, but also? He'd...vanished. The booth was empty. His wine glass sat on the table, half-empty.

"Ah, excuse me, Miss Cavanaugh." Mr. Clicky Heels crisply edged in beside me and handed me the bottle of wine. "It seems your party had somewhere else he needed to be. This is yours now. I thought you might like to take it with you."

My heart sank. Tiarnan had left. He'd seen me stomp out the front door and had given up. This had been the very first date I'd had in so long that I could barely remember what the last one had been like. And I'd blown it.

~

On the way back to my room, a lot of things happened at once. The first thing was Balor and Tiarnan arguing at the bottom of the carpeted staircase in a very animated, and therefore angry, fashion. Hands thrown up in the air, faces screwed up, red dotting their cheeks. The next thing was a deep rumble that shook the floor beneath my feet. And then the deafening roar of an explosion.

I stumbled forward in my heels, more from shock than anything. When another boom shook through the Court, I decided I'd had enough of the damn shoes and kicked them off. By the time I reached the lobby in my bare feet, Balor and Tiarnan had sprung apart, now focusing on the explosions rocking through the Court. Tiarnan's sword was out; Balor had a finger pressed tightly against his eye patch.

"Clark," Balor said, all business now that we were

clearly under attack. "Any idea where those explosions were coming from? Did you see anything?"

Footsteps sounded heavily from behind us, and my heart leapt into my throat. Had our attacker gotten inside? Were they coming for us now? Instinctively, I stepped in front of Balor to block him from whatever came next. Even though I was hardly trained. Even though I had no better weapon than the stilettos in my hand.

I had to protect my Prince.

Duncan flew around the corner, and all the tension released its tight grip on my body.

"We've got a problem," he said, breath ragged.

Balor stepped to the side and edged in front of me. "Yes, I can see that. Where did the explosion come from? Has anyone been hurt?"

"No one's been hurt, but you're not going to like this." Duncan winced. "Brace yourself."

"Stop being cryptic. Tell me what's going on."

"Someone blasted a hole into the dungeon. Right into Lesley's cell. She's gone."

14

"Wait a minute." I shot a look at Balor. "Lesley is *here*? In this House?!"

I'd been told that our friendly neighbourhood serial killer had been locked away in an extremely secure supernatural prison. I hadn't known that she'd been in this very building the entire time. That might have made me feel a teensy bit more uneasy about the whole thing.

"We have very secure cells beneath the Court," Balor said, before turning to Duncan. "Grab Cormac. He might be useful in this scenario. I need you to track her down and bring her back."

Duncan gave a nod and sprinted back down the corridor. Balor turned to Tiarnan next. "I need you to take point guarding the front doors. Moira, go examine the blast. Make sure no one goes anywhere near it. Clark, go tell Elise and Kyle to get on the computers. See if we can make anything out on our CCTV. Which direction she went, who did the blast."

"Okay. And what do you want me to do?"

He clenched his jaw, and then said. "After you've told Elise her orders, join Tiarnan at the door. You're a team now, aren't you? Might as well do something useful with it."

Yikes.

~

Despite my reservations about the whole teaming-up-with-Tiarnan thing, I followed Balor's orders. He didn't even need to use his magical voodoo to make me do it. Things were serious here at Court now. If my Prince gave me an order, I was going to listen. So, while Elise and Kyle watched the security footage, I eased out the front door to join Tiarnan on the marble steps that led up to the veranda and entrance to the Crimson Court. He stood tall and strong as he faced the river, the wind rustling his hair, his hand resting lightly on the hilt of his sword.

"Hi," I said quietly. "Balor told me to join you out here."

"Of course he did."

Wetting my lips, I stepped up to his side and scanned the pavement beyond the front lawn down below us. It wound in front of the River Thames, wrought-iron railings looming above the water. They were empty. For now.

"So, about earlier. Do you want to talk about why you left in the middle of our date?"

He tensed. "I'm not the one who left, Clark. That was you. You know, it's funny. All I wanted was *one* evening. Hell, not even that. A few hours. Just you and me. No Balor Beimnech between us."

"Was that what you two were arguing about before the explosion?"

He shot me a sharp look. "You saw that? Yeah."

"Kind of hard to miss." I sucked in a deep breath, filled my lungs with the cool night air. "Listen, I'm sorry. He showed up outside of the restaurant, and he was extremely agitated. I tried to ignore him at first, but he wouldn't go away. He was creeping around out there. Like a creep. I needed to see what the deal was."

"*Needed* to? Or wanted to?"

I blew out a breath. "Both? He's my Master and my Prince, Tiarnan. We've been working closely together. Plus, the bond between us is incredibly strong, even though I just joined his Court."

"You had some wine tonight. Your bond would have been weakened."

I frowned. "Sure, but—"

"It is more than just the bond. You two have a strange relationship. I won't claim that I could even begin to understand, nor do I think I want to."

I stared at him a moment before responding. "You know what? You're right. It is strange. But my relationship with Balor has nothing to do with you and me. You didn't need to leave tonight. I thought we were having a pretty good time."

"Bloody hell, that's horrific," Tiarnan muttered, tightening the grip on the hilt of his sword.

I frowned at him. "Wow, it really wasn't that bad. If Balor hadn't interrupted, I'm pretty sure our date would have—"

"Not the date," he said, voice going dark. "Look down by the river. Tell me what you see."

I followed Tiarnan's gaze. For a moment, I wasn't entirely sure what he was talking about. A few pedestrians were passing by on the paved walk beside the river. That was normal. They tended to do that day and night, though there'd been far fewer human pedestrians nearby in the past few days, thanks to the news article about Balor's fire.

But one stood out from the rest. And the humans were starting to notice.

A tall, lanky figure with hollowed-out eyes lurched toward us. Her lips were pale, though the last time I'd seen her they'd been painted red. Her shiny shoulder-length hair was now stringy and damp, as if she'd just swam the length of the River Thames.

Water pooled around her bare feet, and she lurched ever forward.

"Shit, that's Maeve," I whispered.

"Looks like the sorcerer has gotten to her," Tiarnan said. "Someone needs to alert Balor. You or me?"

The question felt as though it held far more weight than it should. The mission itself was simple, really. Go inside, find Balor, and tell him what was going on. But it felt like a trap, like Tiarnan was asking something else entirely. So, I gave him an answer that was the opposite of what I truly wanted.

"I'll stay out here and keep an eye on Maeve," I said, fingering the hilt of my sword. "You go find Balor."

On my way back from the command station, I'd grabbed my sword, but I was still very much clad in a tight gold dress and no shoes. Maeve, on the other hand, was now a fae Sluagh. I had no idea what that meant for her powers or what she might be able to do. How strong was she? How fast? If I wounded her, would she even fall?

The additional problem, of course, was that she was a Master in her own right. A leader in Balor's Court. If I killed her, even trying to defend myself, the shit would literally hit the fan. Things between the Houses were already bad enough. We really couldn't afford for them to get any worse. This entire situation was two seconds away from blowing open an actual war.

"Maeve?" I called out to her, hoping that maybe there was a part of her deep beneath the curse of the Sluagh. Of course, that was crazy. The curse was more than just a curse. Only the dead could be turned into Sluaghs, so Maeve was no longer in there, only a shell of who she once was.

She didn't say a word, still stumbling toward me with her pale lips widened into the shape of the moon. Her eyes were vacant, her gaze locked on the building that loomed high behind me. It was like I wasn't even there. Her mission was to get to the Court, and I, somehow, had to stop her.

I drew my sword.

"Put your weapon away, Clark," Balor said from behind me. He strode down the steps, his eyes pinched. He took in the scene. Maeve's eyes, her soaked skin, and the stumble-walk as she continued marching forward.

I lowered my weapon but didn't sheath it, just in case.

"She's focused on the Court. It's like she doesn't even see us," I said. "It makes me think she's intent on getting inside the building."

"And we're going to let her make her way inside. For now." Balor nodded at Tiarnan who stood just inside the doorway with heavy chains hanging from his hands. "The humans are watching, and we don't want to make a scene out here. As soon as she's inside, we'll trap her."

"Trap her?" I gaped at him. "And then what? Your dungeon has been blown to shreds. Besides, you can't just keep a Master of a House hostage, can you? Even if she is a Sluagh? What will the other Masters think?"

Balor's single red eye zeroed in on me. "We're going to trap her, and then we're going to take her somewhere safe where she can't harm herself or anyone else."

"And then what?" I demanded.

"To be honest, Clark, I don't know."

~

After they trapped Maeve in the lobby of the Court, Balor asked Tiarnan to keep an eye on her while we parsed out a plan. Balor and I took up space in his office, out of earshot of any curious fae. For now, he didn't want the news about Maeve to break to the rest of the Court. It would cause too much panic.

I was feeling kind of panicky myself.

Sluaghs were one thing. Vampire Sluaghs were even worse. But fae Sluaghs? I shivered. I didn't even want to think about the damage they could cause.

Balor tapped his chin and then strode over to his corner bar. He poured me a shot of gin, and then whiskey for himself. "We have a dilemma."

"I already know what you're going to say. We have a very dangerous supernatural in our Court, but we can't harm her in any way. The political situation is too tricky for that."

Balor raised an eyebrow. "Good. You're catching on fast, Clark."

I wasn't entirely sure that was a good thing. Politics? Not really something I wanted to be good at.

I tipped the gin down my throat, sighed at the burn. "So, what are you going to do? Talk to the other Masters before doing anything about it?"

Balor clucked his tongue. "A month ago, I would have. Things have changed since then. Fionn would likely attempt to use the situation to trap me. I can't trust anything he says."

"And the Master of the Scottish Court, Athaira?"

Balor shook his head. "She has wanted independence from the Crimson Court for over a decade now. There'll be no help from her."

"So, why not just do whatever you think is best? You're the Prince. They answer to you, not the other way around."

He arched a brow. "That's an interesting sentiment, coming from you."

My cheeks flushed. I hadn't exactly been the picture of obedient, subservient subject since joining the Crimson Court. I didn't really like following rules. Seemed a lot of fae didn't like following them either.

"You know what I mean. I thought Masters were

supposed to follow the lead of their Prince. If you call to them for help..."

"It's not as easy as that, I'm afraid. I could call, and they would likely come, but Fionn and Athaira would want nothing more than to see me sabotaged. This would be a perfect opportunity for that." Balor fell silent, his eyebrows furrowed. "This old vampire Sluagh you tracked down. You're absolutely certain it was the same female?"

"I mean, she was a pile of ash when we found her, and there weren't photographs back then to compare her to...but yeah? It seems that way. Kyle is pretty certain about it, and he's no muppet."

"Right." Balor gave a grave nod. "That settles it then."

"That settles what then?" My heart thumped at the look on his face. Equal parts resigned and angry. He also had that spark in his eye again, the one that made me fear him and want him at the same damn time. I had a feeling that I was not going to like what he'd decided.

"There's something I have to do, and I'm going to need your help." He levelled his gaze at me. "And I'm going to need you to put aside our arguments from earlier. Otherwise, this could all go very wrong."

My mouth went dry. "Balor, you're starting to scare me."

"We cannot kill Maeve, and we cannot leave her bound up in this Court. She's far too dangerous. We need to take her somewhere safe. Somewhere underground until we can find the sorcerer who did this to her and force him to undo the curse."

"Undo it? Is that even possible?"

"I don't know. But I intend to find out." Balor sucked in a deep breath, rested his hand on my shoulder, and looked deeply into my eyes. My bare toes curled against the floor, and my heart skipped a beat. His fingers tightened around my arm, and his eyes dropped to my lips. For a moment, I could have sworn he was going to kiss me. Tension charged through the air, punching against me so hard that I felt like I might collapse underneath the weight of it.

"I know we've had our differences lately, Clark, but I need you to help me with this. And you must swear on your mother's grave that you will not speak a word of this to anyone else."

I blinked and stepped back, like I'd been slapped. *My mother's grave?* Heart racing, I forced myself to stare deep into his eye. Had he discovered something? Had his contact found out more about my past? No, that was impossible. If he had, his reaction would be a hell of a lot stronger than this.

"Before I agree to this, you're going to have to tell me where we're taking her."

"We have to lock her up inside the catacombs."

15

"You want to take her into the catacombs?" My voice came out a screech, and my words bounced against his aged wooden walls. Balor frowned. Clearly, he'd expected me to take this a lot better, but he was wrong. Way wrong.

"It is the safest place for her. We don't yet know how the Sluagh curse affects supernatural bodies. Humans cannot adapt to it. If they spend too much time above ground, they disintegrate. The vampire you and Kyle tracked down somehow survived all these years, but it seems like an isolated case. We can't risk losing her to this curse."

"I get you. I understand. It makes sense. But the catacombs? I don't know how I feel about going back there."

I'd been to the West Norwood Catacombs once before. It was hidden deep within a cemetery and closed to the public. For good reason. The place was creepy as hell and home to hundreds of moist, rotting, rusted coffins. Oh, and it was pretty popular with Sluaghs, as I'd accidentally discovered.

"The Sluaghs who were there are dead now, Clark. There's nothing to fear. Besides, you'll be with me."

I had to roll my eyes at that, even though it did make me feel just a teensy bit better. If we ran into any Sluaghs while we were down there, he wouldn't let them kill me. Of course, that all depended on whether or not we killed each other first.

"Fine. I'll go with you," I said, hating myself for agreeing to this insane mission. There had to be a better way. I just couldn't think of what it was. "Even though I don't understand why you want me to join you. Surely one of the more experienced guards would be a better choice. I know my fighting skills have improved, but I have a long way to go."

"It's not a compliment. I want you to go with me so that I can keep my eye on you."

I glared at him. What the hell did that mean?

∾

Balor "allowed" me to change out of my dress and into something much more appropriate for sneaking into a Sluagh-infested dungeon. Instead of rocking up into the catacombs with bare legs, I slid into a pair of dark trousers that would melt into the night. On top, I wore a thin, long-sleeved shirt and a leather jacket. My boots, also black, were heavy and firm, perfect for kicking arse. And, of course, I had my sword.

Balor was dressed much the same, from the jacket

to the boots to the sword. We were kind of matching. I wasn't sure how I felt about that.

As we headed out into the darkness of the night, I couldn't help but ask him a question that had been on my mind these past few days. "Why do you carry your sword when you have an eye that burns pretty much anything to the ground?"

"I don't always want to win fights by burning things, Clark. Sometimes a sword is the better option. Or fists."

Speaking of fists, Balor wrapped his hands tight around the metal chain that held Maeve between us. We scurried out the back entrance of the Court, hoping no one would spot us. The front of the building, which was most well-known and visible to the public eye, sat facing the River Thames. For years, the paparazzi had camped outside, hoping to get a shot of the elusive Prince. I'd always wondered how he got in and out of the building without being seen. Of course, I hadn't ever imagined finding out this way.

With a fae Sluagh trailing behind me, trapped by a thick metal chain.

On the back side of the building, there was a small alley that had been hidden within the small spaces between walls. It was covered with a large metal roof to camouflage it from any helicopters passing overhead. At one end of the alley sat a bank of black cars. On the other end sat a tall metal gate that looked far sturdier than even the bars of Alcatraz.

"This exit is not known to many," Balor said, tugging Maeve forward. "Moira and Duncan. Kyle. Don't share it with the others."

"Why are you letting me in on your secret escape

hatch? Don't tell me you actually think I'm worthy of levelling up my guard status."

Balor scowled. "I would have rather not told you at all, but I see no way around it. We can't let the humans get wind of this new development. They're already on edge enough as it is."

I'd never been big on the whole 'hide things from the humans to keep them safe' philosophy. Hell, part of the reason I'd started my podcast was so that I could share my interactions with supernaturals with the world. Sure, part of it was to make a living. I'd had a hunch early on that such a specialty show was likely to bring in some cash. But I'd also wanted to give humans some insight into how things worked. They were curious and wary, and I wanted to show them that supes? A lot of them weren't much different than humans, particularly where their love lives were concerned.

All that said, it was difficult to disagree with Balor on this one. We weren't dealing with a romantically-scorned vampire. We had a fae, a powerful one, who had been transformed into a member of the walking dead. Humans knew about vampires, shifters, and fae, but we hadn't told them about Sluaghs. People were going to freak, if they found out.

It was better if they didn't know.

Balor pushed a button on his key fob, and a black SUV beeped. "Help me get her into the backseat of the car."

I opened the door and grabbed Maeve's right arm, gently pulling her across the leather seat. So far, Maeve hadn't shown any signs of typical Sluagh activity. She wasn't lunging for us, she'd kept her teeth firmly inside of her own mouth, and her eyes, while hollow, still held some sign of life. That said, I didn't trust her.

After we'd situated her in the backseat with the chains linked around the seatbelt, Balor and I took our places in the front. He started the engine, pressed another button, and the metal gates swung wide open before us. Balor inched the car out into the alley, swung left, and then quickly filed into traffic.

He was smooth and quick, like our whole secret agent thing was just like any other day on the job. He must have done this same exact move dozens of times before.

As Balor turned the nose of the car down the street, he settled back into the seat. He had visibly relaxed since we'd left the Court, like the hard part of the night was already over. I had a sinking feeling it wasn't.

"I appreciate you coming with me, Clark. Even if you didn't want to."

"I didn't think I had a choice. You Prince. Me subject."

"Yes, well." He sighed and spun the wheel toward the left. "You could have said no."

I shifted on the leather seat, facing him. "I was under the impression that I could never say no to you. That's the whole point of the bond, isn't it? I also recall several times when the magic has pretty much forced me to follow orders."

The silhouette of his jaw rippled, highlighted by the flickering glow of the city lights outside his window. "The point of the bond is to allow a Master to form connections with the fae he serves. There are so many of you. We need to feel that anchor, that link, that reminder of what we are protecting."

Balor's mask was gone now, in the quiet of this car, with no one to overhear his softly spoken words except for me. Oh, and the Sluagh in the backseat. She didn't really count. Probably.

Balor had never really shared how he viewed the Court and his place within it as the ruler. But his words made sense in a very strange, supernatural way. Without a personal connection to each and every one of us, we would just become nothing more than a sea of unfamiliar faces to the Prince.

And unfamiliar faces made selfishness easy.

"As hard as it is for you to believe, Clark, I do not like to compel my fae to do my bidding."

"But you do it anyway," I pointed out.

"Yes." He gave a nod. "If I must. But not always."

Sighing, I leaned back in my seat. "And now we have a sorcerer threatening the existence of the Court. If that message is to be believed, he's not going to stop anytime soon."

"No, I don't believe he will."

"So, what are we going to do? The trail has gone cold. We have no idea who he is or where he's hiding. Or who he's going to target next. Obviously, he's going after fae now. Is he going to try to kill us with our own kind?"

"That is a distinct possibility." Balor tightened his grip on the steering wheel. "And I'm not certain what to do. I've made mistakes in the past when confronting issues like this. Mistakes I am not proud of. It's been years, but those mistakes still haunt me now. I don't want to make the same mistake twice."

His expression had gone raw and open in the moments he'd been speaking. Even in the darkness, I could see the haunted look in his eye. It was as if he'd travelled into the past, somewhere very far from the here and now, away from me. It was the most vulnerable I'd ever seen him, and it shook me to my very core.

Balor Beimnech was as far from vulnerable as I'd ever seen. And, if he was scared, I knew I should be, too.

"What mistakes?" I asked softly.

He let out a shuddering breath and turned the wheel. "It does not matter. It was a long time ago, and I will never again let something like that happen. Not on my watch, not under my command. That is why we must keep Maeve safe, despite her condition. We cannot let tensions between the Courts escalate."

So, whatever incident Balor was referring to had something to do with tensions between the Courts. War, most likely. That could refer to a lot of things and a lot of different time periods. Balor had been Prince for a very long time, and the fae Courts had not always been at peace.

"Ah, here we are." Balor pulled the SUV into a car park on the northern edge of the cemetery. There was a closed gate separating us from the dead within and the thick limbs rising high into the sky. My heart began to thrum just seeing the place. I'd been scared out of my mind last time I'd been here. Not only had I stumbled upon the dead bodies of the missing fae, but I'd been trapped inside a cage with them while the Sluaghs clawed at the bars.

That would make anyone a little jumpy.

Together, Balor and I hauled an eerily silent Maeve out of the back seat and pulled her across the car park until we reached the gates. They were locked, of course, with a thick metal that would take a lot more than a crowbar to manage.

"How are we going to scale the fence with this one?" I jerked my thumb over my shoulder at Maeve. Moonlight streamed along her hair, highlighting the sunken cheekbones of her face.

"We're not. Now, don't panic." Balor lifted his eye patch. Bright light stormed into the night air. I was temporarily blinded by the strength of it. When my vision finally cleared, Balor was hacking away at the charred remains of the lock. It fell to the ground with a clunk.

"Huh," I said. "I guess that'll do."

"See. My power is not scary. It is very useful."

"I agree that it's useful. But it's also very scary, especially when you use it to burn down buildings." I watched as he pulled open the creaking gate, my hands tight around the metal chain.

"*One* building. And please, let's not rehash this argument again. Nor the one we had outside of the restaurant."

"I didn't mention the restaurant."

"No, but you were going to."

"We really do have a lot of arguments, don't we?"

"More than I've had with anyone I've ever met." He frowned. "Except for Fionn. He probably takes the cake."

I arched a brow. "Consider that a challenge."

Still, I decided to try out this new-found peace thing with Balor, as per his request. He was right, as much as I hated to admit it. We couldn't be distracted by arguments if we were going to take a dead fae walking down into the catacombs.

Because if we weren't careful, we might not make it out alive.

16

The clanking chain was the only sound in the cemetery. Not a single bird chirped in the midnight air, and the combination of thick brush and stone crypts sheltered us from the cloying sounds of the city. The honking cars, the murmur of conversation, the whoosh of wheels on slick pavement. Our footsteps were even quiet, the soles of our boots padding silently across the dirt-packed ground.

After pushing our way through the cemetery, we reached the crumbling steps that led down into the abandoned catacombs. Balor took the lead as we descended into darkness, one hand clasped tight around the chain and the other around his sword. I followed suit, sucking in one last fresh breath of night air before entering the mildew-stained, dank, dark ground.

Droplets of water plonked onto the stone ground as we ducked inside. It had rained the day before, and a small carpet of water stretched out before us. Balor gave a nod and splashed forward, further into darkness.

Something smelled odd in here, a scent I couldn't put my finger on. More like a chemical than mould.

"Do you have a tight hold on her chain?" Balor asked, his voice echoing down the dark tunnel. "I'm going to get us some light."

Before I could respond, he'd dropped his end of the chain, leaving me to control Maeve's movements all on my own. Dumb idea, if the fae Sluagh had been at all interested in trying to escape. One tug, and she'd be free from me. I was getting stronger, but I had nothing on a centuries-old Master faerie.

Luckily, she seemed content to just stand there.

As I watched Balor curl his free hand into a strong fist, I couldn't help but notice how powerful he looked, even when there were no lights to illuminate his muscular frame. His outline alone glowed with the kind of magic that was impossible to ignore. I wanted to reach out toward it. I wanted to feel it underneath my hands.

Light rippled from Balor's fingertips, and the tall central gallery of the catacombs roared into view. Not much had changed since the last time we'd been here. The strange, rusted metal bed still sat in the very center of the place, and dank mildew climbed up the walls. There were six corridors that split off from this main one, each leading to stores upon stores of rotting coffins.

"You have the power to make light, too?" I shook my head. "Not fair."

"I am a Prince," was his only explanation.

A scuffling sound whispered from somewhere deep

within this place, and my skin answered by pointing every hair toward the ceiling. "Alright. We've brought Maeve down here. Mission accomplished. Time to go, I think."

"No," Balor said, seemingly oblivious to the utter creeptastic nature of this place. "We need to attach the chain to something. That or find a cell to put her inside. Otherwise, she might wander back up those steps. We cannot have her loose in London."

Truthfully, Maeve didn't look like she was about to wander anywhere. She had started swaying back and forth now, the whole ordeal of her curse obviously taking its toll on her fragile body. She might be fae, but the curse was still a curse, and it rotted a body from the inside out. Once this magic was done with her, she'd turn to ash just like the vampire had.

"Fine," I said. "Let's just chain her to that platform there."

Balor frowned in the direction of the vaulted metal bed. I expected he would argue. He always did. But instead, he gave a nod. "That will do."

With his lighted hand raised in the direction of the table, we inched our way through the water-logged floor. The chemical scent deepened, clawing at my nostrils. A chill sunk deep into my feet as the icy water soaked through my boots. My teeth even began to chatter, but I held tight to the chain.

"Do you smell that?" I asked. "What is it?"

Balor kept moving forward. "I'm not sure. Perhaps whatever flooded this place knocked something loose."

How lovely. So, we could be walking through who knew what.

We reached the metal structure within moments.

Up close, I could see a lot more detail than I had spotted from across the room. There were two chains attached to the strange bed, one on each end. They rose high into the ceiling above, disappearing into darkness. I tipped back my head and looked up. What the hell was this thing?

"That's how they lowered the corpses down here," Balor said when he caught me staring up at the ceiling. "Back when they actually used these catacombs."

I would have asked him how he knew, but he'd probably been alive here in London to see it all happen.

"Is it weird?" I asked him as we wound the chain around the structure. "Watching so many different lives come and go? Are the memories hard to hold onto when so many years pass you by?"

Balor pulled the chain tight and then clasped it into place. "That's an interesting question. Yes, and no. It is both strange and not strange at the same time. I've become used to it. It is the way the world works for us. That said, there are times when I'm struck by just how many years I have existed in this world. At times like these, when I can clearly see the wear and tear the years have had on the world. Sometimes, in London, it's more difficult to notice that. There's been so much progress. It's so loud, so vibrant. The city sparkles and shines, but not everywhere."

I felt that. I really did. For once, Balor's words resonated with me in a way they never had. Maybe he and I could understand each other better someday.

"I would ask for some stories of past Londons, but I kind of figure that standing in the middle of a puddle, surrounded by the dead and a weird fae zombie probably isn't the right time."

Balor laughed. He actually laughed. It was smooth and baritone, a sound that sent shivers all along my skin. A comfortable, safe sort of sound I wanted to wrap myself inside of and never leave. I wasn't sure I'd ever heard him laugh before and certainly not like this. I decided right then and there that I needed to try to make him do it more often.

That was when the scuffling started. A rustle of leaves against water. The rush of footsteps echoing off the dank walls.

And the scent of death that quickly followed.

I froze, swallowing hard. Every hair on my skin stood on end, and my heart beat so hard that I swore it was trying to punch its way out of my chest. The sound grew louder, louder, louder, until it felt as though the entire world was closing in all around us.

"The dead are coming," I whispered. I couldn't see them yet, but I knew. We—and by we, I mean Balor—might have killed the Sluaghs that had been in the catacombs before, but there were more now. And they had heard us.

"Probably it's time to get out of here," I said because I wasn't certain that Balor had heard my choked words about the dead.

He dropped the chain, lifted his sword, and motioned for me to rush to his side. I whirled around the structure, joining him just in time to see about twenty Sluaghs stumble-walk their way out of the furthest corridor. Even after having seen them several times already, I still shuddered when my gaze caught on their tall, lanky, bone-riddled forms. They lurched forward, stringy hair hanging down into their sunken faces. Eyes open wide, they stared right at us, but there was nothing behind their gaze. No life, no heart, no soul. Nothing but hunger.

Hunger for us.

And there was kind of a big problem with our situation. They were between us and the exit.

"What are we going to do?" I whispered under my breath. Not entirely sure why I bothered. It wasn't like it would matter if they heard me. They would still come.

"It looks as though we're going to have to fight them, Clark. Stay behind me as much as you can. When I shout to run, you need to run." Balor shifted in front of me, his fingers still flickering with bright orange light. I stared hard at his muscular back, at the tension in his frame. My heart thumped hard. We might have had our differences, but I was still bound to him. And what was more, he was bound to me. As my Prince, he would do anything to protect me, even sacrifice himself.

I couldn't let him do that. I wouldn't let him fight them by himself.

"Let me help you," I said, voice trembling. "Moira has been training with me. I can fight."

"Not necessary. As soon as they get close enough, I'll use my power against them."

Suddenly, that strange scent got a hell of a lot stronger. Hard and metallic, biting through the mouldy, damp earthiness that had been there only seconds earlier. I sniffed the air, frowning. What the hell *was* that? And why did it seem so familiar?

"Petrol," Balor said in a low growl. "That's petrol, Clark."

My heart lurched in my chest. "Oh my god, you're right. But—"

"The sorcerer knew we would come here, and he rigged this place for our arrival." He lifted his boot, sniffing at the water. "It's a trap."

Bloody bastard.

Wetting my lips, I inched up toward Balor's side, and he did nothing to try to stop me. The dead were only a few meters away now, and we had no defence but our swords and our fists. Balor couldn't use his eye to get us out of this one. If he did, the entire place would be blown to shreds, including us.

Balor shot one last glance my way. "Don't attack forward. Wait until one comes to you. Go for their weapons first. Disarm them. Then, go for the head."

He didn't have time to tell me more than that.

The Sluaghs reached us. Three stood in front of the rest. Balor dropped the light from his hand, gripped his sword between both palms, and swung. His blade made contact with the first Sluagh, slicing straight through sinew and bone. A sickening crunch joined the sounds of boots splashing through water doused with petrol. I swallowed hard and stood my ground, and then a Sluagh turned my way.

Its sunken eyes seemed to look past me, as if it were staring deep into the abyss of a different world. Gritting my teeth, I swung my sword at its arm before it could make a move against me. The steel sliced through its skin, but the Sluagh barely seemed to blink. Its strange, thin lips twisted up into a grimacing smile, and then it threw its sword right at my face.

I ducked down, throwing out my legs to catch it off balance. The Sluagh crashed to the floor. Before it could react, I took my blade and shoved it straight into its neck. The end sunk deep into its flesh, and dark red poured out of the wound, coating its skin and the water-logged ground beneath it.

I stared down at the Sluagh, my heart hammering so hard that I could barely hear anything else over the roar of it inside of my head. My veins pulsed, the scent of iron filled the air. Every cell in my body felt alive, like a strange magic had filled my gut, flooding my blood with the electricity of the fight.

Yanking my sword out of the Sluagh, I looked up at my next attacker. Everything in the catacombs suddenly became crisp and clear, as if someone had turned on the overhead lights. I glanced at Balor, expecting him to have gathered the light around his hand again, but he was still thick inside of the fight.

It wasn't coming from him.

Hell, it wasn't coming from anywhere.

Balor disposed of another enemy, the body crashing with a splash onto the ground. He wiped his forehead and glanced over his shoulder to check on me. He froze, eyes open wide. "Clark?"

That was when a Sluagh slowly stood behind him, mangy hair hanging down in its face, mouth twisting into a brutal smile. And then the Sluagh slammed the blunt end of his sword right on top of Balor's head.

17

The world slowed around me as Balor fell. His body, so strong and so powerful, crashed hard onto the ground. The Sluagh's grin widened, and he held his sword higher over his head. Two seconds and that sword would connect with Balor's neck, and my Prince would be dead forever.

I flew into action. I didn't think. I didn't consider. I didn't plan. My body took over along with the fae magic that bubbled deep within me.

Adrenaline charging through my body, I threw my feet forward. A deep guttural roar tore from my throat, just as my entire vision turned to red. I wouldn't let this Sluagh kill Balor. My Master, my Prince, the fae who had pledged his life to protect mine, and I had done the same for him. My steel connected with steel, just in time, with the force of my own swing so strong that it knocked the Sluagh back. He flew several meters away from me, falling to his knees.

My heart beating wildly, I slowed to a stop and

stared at the shocked Sluagh. Hell, I was just as shocked. And then I took a look at the ten other Sluaghs lurching forward just behind him, and then at the crumbling steps toward safety. They were still between us and the only way to get the hell out of here.

It was a split second decision. A fully gut-defining moment.

I knelt down, grabbed Balor from underneath his armpits, and dragged him several steps to the left until we were safe inside the nearest cage. He was heavy, and it took all my strength to slide him the short distance across the slick ground. But I did it. Somewhere deep inside of me, I'd found the ability to do far more than I'd ever thought.

The Sluagh who I'd knocked back realised what I was doing two seconds too late. I slammed the door to the gate behind me and locked it into place.

Of course, that meant that I was now trapped inside the catacombs while hungry Sluaghs tried to get at my flesh. Again. I really didn't like that I kept getting myself into these kinds of situations.

Ignoring the Sluaghs clutching at the bars, I dropped to my knees on the wet ground and leaned down to see if I could find a pulse in Balor's neck. There was no way in hell he, of all fae, could have been taken down that easily, but—

"Clark," he murmured, cracked open his eye. "Why does it look like you've trapped us inside the catacombs with the Sluaghs?"

I let out a hollow laugh of relief, my shoulders slumping forward. Pulling back, I stared down at him. He blinked up at me, strangely vulnerable for once.

Not that he stayed that way for long. A second later, he slowly pushed himself up from the ground and glared out at the hungry Sluaghs. There were dozens of them out there now. His wet, petrol-soaked shirt clung to the muscles in his back, highlighting every ridge, every dip, every rippling…

Damn it, Clark. Get a grip!

"Sorry. I didn't know what else to do. Maybe I panicked a bit."

He sighed and placed a hand against his head, wincing. "No, this is fine. They'll either give up and go away, or we'll fight our way out. I just need to wait for my head to heal or I won't be able to see straight for the fight. It took a pretty hard hit against the floor."

He did look a little worse for wear. He was swaying a bit, kind of like Maeve, who was watching this entire ordeal where she was still chained to the metal structure, a strange blank expression on her face.

"Just sit down for now." Moving to his side, I clasped his elbow and helped lower him back to the ground. "How are you going to heal? Don't you need Deirdre for that?"

A smug smile flickered across his face, but it wasn't nearly as annoying as it normally was, not when he looked like he was two seconds away from passing out. "I can heal myself. I just need some time. It would help if…never mind."

"It would help if what?" My heart began to race, even if I had no idea what he was talking about. There was just something in the tone of his voice. Something deep and dark. Something that made my insides feel as if they might twist up into a pretzel.

Whatever he wanted me to do...I probably wasn't going to like it. Or maybe I would like it too much.

"Since healing is not one of my innate powers, it can be difficult, particularly since my body is cold. It would help to have some...assistance."

His body was cold. So, what the hell did that mean?

He continued, "Normally I would use my eye to fix the issue, but since we're standing in the middle of a crypt that is rigged to blow, that's not an option."

At that, he pulled his shirt over his head. My eyes widened. The strength of his body was even more impressive without a pesky shirt in the way. The ridges of his abs were cut deep, his stomach curving into a perfect V that disappeared into his low-slung trousers. His skin was golden and smooth, save for a small smattering of hair around his belly button. I knew I was staring. And I also knew that my hot cheeks were probably the color of blood.

"Come here," he said in a low growl as if he could sense my hesitation, and my desire. Which...he probably could. My body had gone tense, and my heart raced fast. Hell, he could probably smell my reaction to him. An intense combination of fear and want and need so great that I could barely breathe.

"What is it that you want me to do?" I whispered the words, refusing to take a step forward. Not yet, anyway.

"Skin on skin contact. It will heat me, and I will be able to draw some extra power from you."

I wet my lips. "You want to draw power from me? You can do that?"

"Oh, yes." His mouth turned up into a delicious

smile. "Every Master can draw power from his fae. It's not a power I use very often, but I rarely find myself in this situation. Now, stop stalling. Come here, Clark."

My heart hurt from how hard it thumped against my ribs. Slowly, I crossed the room toward him, my feet sloshing against the water. I told myself that the sooner I helped him heal, the sooner we could be out of this hellhole. The Sluaghs were still clustered around the entrance to the cage where we were trapped. They clawed at the bars, screeched at the need to get close enough to tear us to shreds.

It kind of put a damper on the whole desire part of the equation, which helped.

As I lowered myself to his side, he opened his arms, welcoming me toward him. "You should probably remove your shirt as well."

My neck flushed. "Right."

I slid off my leather jacket, dropped it to the floor, and pulled my black tank top over my head. Balor's eye flashed, even in the dark.

"Good. Now, come here."

The cold air bit at my skin, and the soggy petrol water still soaked deep into my bones. Chill clung to my bare arms and stomach. I could probably use a little body heat myself. Taking a deep breath, I leaned into Balor.

His body brushed against mine, and my core tightened instinctively. Warmth spread through my limbs, and a deep dark magic filled my head. But, I couldn't help but be super aware of how awkward this whole thing was. Balor was sitting on the floor with his back against the wall. I was kind of leaning over him, with my boobs pressed up against his chest, my knees digging into the stone floor.

"Just sit on my lap, Clark. Get comfortable. This could take a little while."

"Do what now?" My voice hitched up at the end.

Amusement peppered his next words. "Sit on my lap. No need to be scared. I won't bite."

Except, I wasn't really afraid of him *biting*…

Still, I did as he said, mostly because I didn't know how long I could stay hunkered over him on my knees like this. I spread my thighs and slid on top of him, my chest against his chest, his face now only centimetres from my own. A slow smile curled across his lips, and another spike of desire shot through my veins.

"Good." He wrapped his arms around my back and pulled me closer to him. The skin of our chests were now so tightly pressed against each other that it almost felt as if they'd melted into one. The warmth of him engulfed me. I wasn't entirely sure how he could have been cold. He was practically an inferno, lighting me up both outside and within. Despite my every attempt to keep myself together, I just couldn't. Not when we were so close. Not when I could feel every single inch of him pressed up against me like this. Shuddering, I closed my eyes, wrapped my arms around his neck, and gave in.

Magic pulsed around us, waves and waves of darkness churning like a whirlwind. It bit at my skin, sunk into my bones, and made my mind reel from the force of it. He groaned, a sound that lit a million fires deep within my core. I wanted to respond, to let him know that I felt everything he felt, that I wanted nothing more than to stay like this forever.

The Sluaghs had become a distant memory. Their terrible screeching and nails against metal were nothing more than a distant chatter far, far away on the wind. My whole world had become Balor. Balor and no one else.

But it was all too much. The magic was intense. It weighed down my eyelids, made my bones feel like mush. One moment, I was wrapped around my Master, letting him feed on the power of my fae soul. The next moment, I was falling into darkness.

∽

I woke up with my arms wrapped tight around Balor and with my breasts mashed against his muscular chest. My eyes flew open, and I tensed. Oh my god, I'd fallen asleep like this.

"Ah, there you are," he said, his deep voice curling with amusement. "Welcome back."

Slowly, I sat up straighter and pulled back so that I could look into his face. I felt a little bit sheepish about the whole falling asleep thing. "Um, sorry. I have no idea how I fell asleep in the middle of a life-or-death mission, but…sorry."

He smiled. "No need to apologise. I should have warned you. I was drawing on your power. It can sometimes feel quite draining, particularly if you're already tired. Meanwhile, I have just been enjoying the feel of your body against mine."

My hands tightened around his shoulders, and I wet my lips. He followed the movement of my tongue, his gaze hungry and sharp. "Did it heal you?"

"Oh, yes. I am one-hundred percent ready to take

down some Sluaghs." He flicked his eye toward the entrance of the cage. "However, it looks as though they've given up. The magic knocked me out as well. I was still unconscious when they left, or else I would have gone after them."

"Oh. So we can leave now."

Sitting in a petrol soaked cage with a dozen coffins wasn't exactly the sexiest situation I'd ever found myself in, but I suddenly wished we didn't have to go. Balor's mask had fallen away. He had become naked before me. The caring Prince he tried so hard to hide was sitting quite literally underneath me. There was also the fact that he was impossibly hot, and I wanted nothing more than to straddle him for many hours to come.

"Clark." He gripped my chin in his hand and pulled me toward him. My lips crashed against his, and his tongue dipped into my open mouth. I moaned as sparks lit up along every inch of my skin. No matter what had happened between us, I still wanted this. Desperately so.

I slid my hands into his silky hair and pressed myself closer against his body. The apex of my thighs met his, and through our trousers, I could feel him harden beneath me. His kiss deepened, and his hands roamed across my back. I'd thought I was warm before, but that was nothing compared to the heat I felt now.

Everything felt as if it were on fire. Him, me, every cell in my body, the core between my thighs. Was this his magic? His allure? Or was it just the overwhelming desire that churned through my veins?

Suddenly, he pulled back. *Again.* He dropped his

forehead to mine, his chest heaving with belabored breaths. "I am sorry, Clark. I shouldn't have done that. I lost control of myself. It's so easy to do when I'm with you."

My heart squeezed tight, and my voice came out rough. "Why do you keep pulling away from me?"

"I can't tell you." He squeezed his eye shut and turned away. "I can't tell anyone."

18

*B*alor and I drove back to the Court in silence. We'd searched for the Sluaghs in the catacombs, but they weren't there. That meant they'd gone above ground, which was unsettling. They were nowhere to be found in the cemetery either. Maeve was still chained up to the metal bed, swaying back and forth as if in some kind of trance. We'd kind of fulfilled our mission, but we'd also kind of accidentally unleashed some more walking dead onto London's streets.

Things hadn't gone according to plan, exactly.

We were going to have to ramp up the investigation if we wanted to stop the sorcerer before things got too out of hand.

Meanwhile, I was just going to sit in the passenger seat moping about the fact that Balor couldn't figure out what the hell he wanted from me. At first, I'd felt hurt, but I was quickly starting to turn that pain into anger.

"I need to ask you about something," he said quietly, gripping the wheel.

"Let me guess. You want to know if I'll agree that we should have a strict Master and Subject relationship. Again. None of that pesky kissing you hate so much." I glared out the window at the passing streetlamps. "Sure. Fine. Since that's clearly what you want, I have no problem agreeing to it. I do just want to point out one thing. You were the one who pulled me in for the kiss. Stop doing that if you want nothing from me."

"Were you aware of what you did in the catacombs?" he asked, ignoring every single word I'd said about the kiss.

I crossed my arms and glared at him. "What I *did*? You mean, sharing my power with you so that you could heal? Yes, I am very aware of that. You're welcome, by the way."

He shook his head. "No, before that. When we were fighting the Sluaghs."

I frowned. "You mean when I killed one? Yeah, that fight was pretty similar to when I fought the vampire Sluagh in Highgate. I'm stronger and faster than I was before. I think my fae powers are finally kicking in, which is good, right? That's normal when a fae joins a Court."

"Your eyes shifted."

A strange buzz filled my ears as I blinked at Balor. "Say what now?"

"Your eyes, Clark." He shifted on his seat as he shot a glance my way. "They changed. They went black. A black so deep that, for a moment, I thought you'd been transformed into a Sluagh."

Blood roared through my veins, and my body spiked with fear. Had the sorcerer been down there and we hadn't realised it? Had he set a trap not to kill us but to turn us into mindless members of the dead?

"No. Please tell me that's not what's happening. Please tell me I'm not going to become one of them."

"No, no. You're not turning into a Sluagh, Clark." He held up his hand and shook his head. "That was only what your eyes looked like at first. When I got a closer look at them, I realised they were more like an animal's eyes. Did anything happen then? Could you see differently at all?"

I swallowed hard. Actually, I had. At the time, I'd thought it had something to do with Balor's powers or maybe even the Sluagh's. I'd never considered that it had anything to do with me. All my life, I'd never shifted. I'd never even come close. I didn't know how. Could I have accidentally done it without even realising?

"Yes, I could see better. In the dark."

"Well. Then, your fae powers aren't the only ones becoming stronger as your days go by in the Court. We may find out what you can shift into after all. If I were to guess, you might be a fox perhaps. The eyes would match, and they can see well in the dark."

A fox. Clark Cavanaugh shifting into a fox. The idea scared me, but I didn't know why. Foxes could be deadly but not like werewolves or bears. I wouldn't leave behind a trail of bloody bodies in my wake if I were to get out into London while in my shifted state. Still, transforming into an animal would feel like a loss of control. And I didn't like not being in control.

"Shouldn't your Court only enhance the fae side of me? I mean, your magic applies to only fae."

"You're right." He gave a nod. "It does. However, I've never had a half-shifter in my Court, so perhaps this is just how things work for you. And I imagine these powers you're seeing will only grow stronger. Next time you're in a fight, I would bet a hundred quid your eyes will shift again."

Again. Which meant...next time, I might shift even further into the animal within me. And then I really wouldn't have any control. Maybe it was time to reach out to Tiarnan's shifter friend, get a handle on my powers before they got a handle on me.

"So, are we just not going to talk about what happened in the catacombs? And I don't mean the shifting eyes part of it," I said.

His jaw rippled as he clenched his teeth. "There is nothing to talk about, Clark. We just need to be more careful in the future. I want to give in to what I feel for you, but I cannot. And that's all I am willing to say on the matter."

His voice had turned cold and hard once again, the mask firmly back in place. Fine. If that was what he wanted, then so be it. Next time he kissed me, and I knew it would happen, I would be the one who pushed him away.

~

We returned to a Court full of chaos. The human authorities had been called. Whether they had been alerted by the fae inside the building or by humans who had witnessed the explosion, it was hard to know. Police cars and fire trucks were clustered around the smoking section of the building. There were several uniformed humans speaking with Elise and Duncan. A whole crowd had gathered to watch, including some reporters who were recording every moment of the scene.

Balor and I drove by once, and then parked the car in the secure entrance of the building. His hands were gripped tight against the wheel, his gaze focused hard on the pavement in front of the car.

"If anyone asks, we went looking for Lesley. Do not mention Maeve to a single soul."

"Not even the guard—"

"If there is anything that I have learned from recent conflicts, it is that I cannot trust anyone. Do not tell a single soul. Make sure Tiarnan does not speak a word of this to anyone either."

And with that, Balor threw open the door and braced himself for our return to the Court.

Inside, things were just as chaotic. Fae were streaming through the lobby, wringing their hands, eyebrows pinched tight. Moira spotted me as I wandered into the insanity. She stood by one of the marble columns that held up the domed ceiling, most likely keeping an eye on things in case fear escalated into something else.

I joined her by the column. "This looks tense. What are the cops doing here?"

"When there is an explosion, coppers tend to notice. Particularly when we were accused of setting a pub on fire, and now this." She gave my body a full glance over and sniffed. "You smell weird. Where have you been?"

Whoops. I probably should have changed into some non-catacomby clothes before letting anyone within ten meters of me. But there was a crowd between me and the staircase leading up to my room, so I probably wouldn't have made it there anyway. "Balor and I went looking for Lesley. Had to stop for some petrol. I spilled some on my shoes."

She wrinkled her nose. "Gross. Maybe swap those boots for a different pair. I doubt that stuff washes out."

"I'll keep that in mind." I scanned the crowd. The fae were clearly getting restless, and they likely had no idea what the hell was going on. Neither did I, really. "So, what's the news? We didn't find Lesley, but has anyone else? Any idea who exploded her on out of here?"

Moira gave a sharp shake of her head. "Nope. Nothing. On either front. Lesley is long gone it seems, and there's no evidence to suggest who got her out. Whoever did it messed with the cameras again. I mean, the likely culprit is Maeve, what with her disappearing act. Of course, Fionn or Nemain are also options, though I was under the impression those two weren't particularly fond of each other. Not with everything that went down when she first took the throne."

"You mean, when she had the previous Princess killed so she could take over."

"That's right. She's a real piece of work, that one."

"Yes. She is." I pressed my lips firmly together. "You don't think she'd be in London, do you?"

Moira snorted. "Not a chance in hell. Nemain, for all her blustery attitude, would never get her own hands dirty. She always makes others do her shit. Some say it's because she's smart. Others, like me, say it's because she's a bloody coward."

"Careful." Ondine slid up next to us. "Don't let Balor hear you talking about Nemain. He'll blow a gasket. Clark, why do you smell like you've just taken a swim in a pool full of sewage water?"

"Right? She smells like foot fungus."

"Balor and I went to the petrol station and—"

"Wait, shh. Here he comes."

Balor strode into the room. His shirt was still wet, clinging to his chest. Moira turned my way, eyebrow raised. I ignored her look, though I knew my cheeks were pink. Every fae in the room fell silent, all eyes turning for information and comfort from the Master of this House. His eye scanned the crowd, landed on me. For a moment, time seemed to stop. And then he shifted his gaze away.

"Listen, everyone. I know you're all scared and worried about the explosion that happened here tonight. And I cannot blame you." He sucked in a deep breath before continuing. "Someone has made a direct attack on our Court. We have already begun to investigate the matter, and the human authorities have pledged to help us find the culprit. You can rest easy that whoever did this will be behind bars very shortly. Now, go back to your rooms and try to get some sleep tonight. The more—"

"Everyone is saying Lesley escaped. Is that true?" A male violet-haired fae stepped forward, towering over everyone else.

Balor levelled his gaze at the fae. "Yes, that is true. However, we will find her and return her to where she belongs—behind bars. Then, she'll have her trial. Remember, we found her once. We will do it again."

"Return her to where?" another voice sounded from the crowd. "The dungeons were blown up."

"What if she kills some more fae?" shouted another.

The murmur of their voices started rising, along with their thoughts. Despite my ability to block out minds during everyday life, the strength of their fear and their worry began to break through my walls. Gritting my teeth, I lowered my head and pushed toward the staircase. I needed to get out of here, or I'd collapse all over again.

But one voice broke through, above all the rest. "Look at her. She's running. The half-fae can't crack it."

I was just about to whirl on my feet and shout words at the air when Tiarnan appeared at my elbow. He gripped on tight and held me steady, guiding me toward the staircase. One step in front of the other, up, up, up, until the voices began to die away.

Finally, we hit the landing on the next floor.

It was only then that I let out the breath that I'd been holding, slumping against the wall in relief.

"You okay?" Tiarnan asked, his kind eyes searching mine.

"Now I am." I gave him a weak smile. "Thanks for that. Sometimes emotional crowds can be a little tricky to deal with when you're a mind reader."

"I can see that." A pause. "Would you like me to help you to your room?"

"I…"

He frowned and sniffed the air. "Is that petrol?

You and Balor disappeared with Maeve. Where did you go?"

My heart began to thump hard. Tiarnan had been nothing but honest with me from the beginning, and I'd repeatedly thrown that right back into his face. I didn't want to lie to him now either, but Balor had made it clear I had no other choice. Looking into Tiarnan's eyes, I couldn't help but wish that things were different. I couldn't help but want to sever that hold that Balor had on me.

Tiarnan was different. Why couldn't that be enough?

"I'm not supposed to tell anyone where we took her."

He sighed and shook his head. "Fine. Listen, I've been wanting to talk to you. I've been thinking about what I said to you earlier, and I think maybe I was wrong."

I blinked at him. "What do you mean?"

"I think maybe I overreacted." He grimaced and glanced at the ground, shoving his hands into his pockets. "About the connection you have with Balor. I mean, he's your Master. Of course you are going to answer to him when he calls. I had that kind of bond with Fionn, too, when he still had me by his side. I was reading way more into it than I should have, and I'm sorry."

My cheeks flamed. If only he knew the full truth of the situation. He wasn't reading too much into it at all. If anything, he wasn't reading *enough* into it. Something about Balor and his stupid allure had snatched me right up. It was more than just our bond. It was a desire I couldn't shake, no matter how hard I tried.

"Tiarnan, you don't have to apologise. I can see how it looked. I probably would have gotten a bit miffed as well if you'd taken off during our date to go talk to someone else."

"Shout." He grinned. "You mean shout at someone else."

"Well, yes," I said, biting back a smile. "I guess you're right about that."

He practically beamed. "So, should I take you back to your room? We can pick up where we left off..."

I heard the suggestion in his words, and if I were any other girl, I probably would have said yes. He was a hot fae warrior with perfect hair and a muscular body that meant he could probably throw me over his shoulder. He was nice. And forgiving. That was a big plus.

But I wasn't some other girl. I was Clark, and only hours earlier I'd straddled someone else, yearning for sex. Someone who was the very opposite of the sweet male standing before me.

So, I sighed and shook my head. "I'm sorry. It's been a long, crazy night, and this whole explosion and Lesley escaping thing kind of just makes me want to curl up with a bar of chocolate and go to bed."

"Ah." His eyes dimmed. "I see."

"But maybe a rain check," I said quickly. "When things calm down."

"When things calm down," he repeated. "Unfortunately for me, it doesn't seem like things calm down around here very often."

19

The next morning, I was awoken by the sound of bulldozers. They were somewhere outside my window, churning deep into the ground and shaking the very foundation beneath my bed. Groggily, I peeled open my eyes and padded over to the window.

At the very corner of my window, I could see that maintenance workers had flooded the scene around the hole. Bright yellow trucks glowed in the darkness. They'd already dug out a substantial portion of the destroyed dungeon, but they still had a long way to go. Sighing, I threw on some clothes and headed down to the command station. I wasn't going to get any more sleep, so I might as well get started with work super early.

We had a sorcerer to catch. And also whoever was launching attacks on our House.

Everyone else had already beaten me down there. None of them looked the worse for wear, but Elise was visibly yawning. I probably looked like a raccoon, which was great, since Balor was looking just as perfect as he always did. And he was studiously avoiding my gaze. Also fun.

"Morning, Clark." Moira passed me a coffee. "I saved this for you, but you actually don't look like you need it today. For once, you're looking pretty chirpy. Nice sleep?"

"Huh. That's weird, because I feel like death warmed over." I greedily took the coffee from her hands and took a large gulp of the sweet, sweet caffeine. Closing my eyes, I sighed and smiled. "God, that's good. Thanks for this. I definitely need it. The bulldozers and all that." Plus, I'd tossed and turned all night, nightmares about Lesley churning through my mind.

She was out there in the world, doing who knew what.

She'd gone after me, Ondine, Tiarnan, and Balor already. Would she come after us again?

And, this time, would I be able to take her down?

She'd underestimated me before. I didn't think she would again.

"Well, at least you don't smell like a car engine this morning." She cracked a smile and elbowed me in the side. "Did Tiarnan help with that?"

The entire room fell silent. Balor shifted toward me, and I felt the intensity of his red eye move across every inch of my face. Elise cleared her throat. Kyle tapped harder on the keys, like that would make this entire thing less embarrassing. The only relief in all of this was that Tiarnan himself wasn't in the command station.

"Actually, yes. He did help with that." I stared at

DEAD FAE WALKING

Balor, waiting to see his reaction. Absolutely zero muscles in his face moved.

"We need to focus on the task at hand," he said instead, pointing at a map of the building that had been laid out on the table. "We need to determine how this happened, who did it, and then we need to track them down. Meanwhile, we also need to determine potential locations for Lesley. Perhaps she's returned to America, but I doubt it."

I arched an eyebrow. "She'd be stupid to stick around."

"Unless she plans on doing something else," Elise murmured, her hands curled around a steaming mug like it was a lifeline.

"What about the sorcerer?" I asked. "Lesley's escape sucks and all, but don't forget we have a dead-raising maniac at large, too."

"Kyle's working on that. If the sorcerer is collecting Sluaghs, as it seems he is, there won't be very many places in this city where he can do that unnoticed. In return for our help on a few human cases, the police have agreed to alert us of any suspicious reports."

"Unfortunately," Kyle said, pulling a tab on a soda can, "there are about three hundred of these reports from the past two days. Ever since the fire at the pub, supernatural reports have skyrocketed. It's going to take awhile to comb through all these."

"I can help," I said. This was exactly the kind of project that I could really sink my teeth into right now. Papers, files, reports. No swords or undead vampires, thanks.

Tiarnan flew into the command station, his chest

heaving with belabored breaths. His eyes were wild; his hair skewed this way and that. Red dotted his cheeks. Unease churned through me as he slowed to a stop in the center of the floor.

"Tiarnan." Balor strode away from the computers, frowning. "What's going on?"

He shook his head slowly back and forth and moved his mouth, almost like he couldn't form the words. "You're going to have to come see this."

I furrowed my eyebrows. Clearly, whatever he wanted to show us wasn't good, but it couldn't be that bad, could it? I'd neither heard nor felt any explosions, and it was the bloody crack of dawn. Bad things, as I'd quickly come to realise, didn't tend to happen at five in the morning. It was one perk of being a new member of the early bird club.

We trailed out behind Tiarnan, following him down the corridor in the opposite direction of the main lobby. He came to a stop just outside of Balor's office. That unease I'd felt before? It was much more intense now. Why the hell had he taken us here of all places?

"I, ah..." He ruffled his hair. "Sorry about this, Balor. I saw her and locked her up in here before anyone else could see her." He pointed at the chair he'd jammed under the knob. "I didn't know where else to take her."

Balor lifted an eyebrow and slid the chair out from underneath the doorknob. He motioned for all of us to get behind him. We did as we were told, although every single cell in my body wanted to stand between Balor and whatever Tiarnan had trapped inside.

Balor pushed the door open, a finger grazing

against the bottom side of his eye patch. Lesley stood just inside his office, shambling around like she was lost. She spun in slow circles, her eyes vacant, wide, and as dark as her soul. Fear tumbled through my gut.

She was a Sluagh.

Balor quickly closed the door and slid the chair back under the knob. His expression reflected absolutely nothing about how he felt. "You did well in bringing her to my office. It's best if the rest of the Court does not see this for now."

Duncan arched a brow. "You don't seem surprised."

"That is because I am not." Balor glanced my way before continuing. "Clark and Tiarnan encountered another fae zombie while we were standing guard out front last night. We decided to take her away from the Court, where she could not harm anyone."

"Ah. That makes a lot more sense than the other thing I thought," Moira said, shooting a glance my way. "When you and Clark disappeared...well, nevermind."

Tiarnan frowned. "Why didn't you tell the rest of the guards? That's important information, Balor. If there are fae Sluagh running around, the members of the Court should know."

"Watch your tone, Fianna," Moira warned, taking a step toward Tiarnan as she placed her hand on the hilt of her sword. "He might not be your Master, but he's taken you in under his wing. When the boss wants to keep information to himself, it's for good reason. Respect that."

Tiarnan merely glowered at Moira in response.

"I did not want to cause a panic," Balor said. "It

was my mistake to think it was a one-off situation. Where did you find her?"

"Wandering around in the hallway," Tiarnan said.

Balor frowned. "Who was on duty last night and this morning?"

"Humans," Duncan said, clearing his throat. "The cops said they wanted to keep an eye on things, so I let them."

A chill swept down my spine. Oh, shite. That was not a good sign. If the humans had been on guard when the Sluagh had come…we all rushed back down the hallway to the front door of the Court. On the front veranda, lit up by the morning sunlight, were three bloodied corpses of human cops.

My stomach tumbled over itself, and nausea bubbled in my throat. Blood was everywhere. Their skin had been slashed to shreds, and chunks of their arms were missing, as if they had been partially eaten.

I threw a hand over my mouth and twisted away. Tears stung my eyes. This was too much. Whoever had done this had to be stopped. We had to find this sorcerer before any more innocent lives were lost.

"Motherfucker," Moira muttered before picking up one of the cop's discarded batons and then tossing it onto the ground.

I glanced up at the chug of a ferry through water. One of the early morning boats churned through the river. The bank was quiet this early, and the riverside path was clear, but it wouldn't be for long. Humans would be out soon, taking an early run or hurrying to meetings for work. Plus, the usual gawkers. They usually didn't get here until later in the day, but they would come, too.

And we had three murdered policemen on our front stoop.

"Boss, what should we do?" Duncan asked quietly. Even his usual steadfast big-guy bravado had disappeared. "There are some cops on the opposite side of the building, where the diggers are clearing out the dungeon."

Balor shoved a hand into his dark, silver-streaked hair. He closed his eye, muttering underneath his breath too low for any of us to hear. Whether he was cursing the world or whispering some kind of fae prayer, I couldn't tell. A part of me wanted to reach out toward his mind, to see if I could hear him when his mental defences would be so low. But I held back.

"We must tell them," Balor finally said, his voice so resigned that it sent a chill to the very depths of my bones.

"Can I put forth an objection to that?" Tiarnan asked, edging closer. "We had a similar situation at our House once. Vampires attacked the human police outside of our home. They'd come to ask us some questions, as they did often. Anyway, we went straight to the authorities when it happened. The humans ended up blaming us for all of it, even though they couldn't prove it. They even arrested a few of us. Questioned us repeatedly. Two of our fae are still in prison over it, even though they weren't involved at all."

"What?" Balor's gaze went sharp as he turned to look at Tiarnan. "Fionn never told me about this."

"There are many things Fionn has never mentioned to you. He did not want you to get involved. He thought you would take the side of both the vampires and the humans."

"That is ridiculous," Balor said, tone clipped. "My loyalty is to my fae."

"I know that. But many others cannot see the truth, not when you make alliances with shifters and vampires, the very supernaturals who have threatened our existence for centuries."

"And what would you have me do instead?"

"Humans don't know about Sluaghs. If we went forward with this…they would panic. They would blame all of this on us, to hell with the evidence."

"Tiarnan has a point, boss," Duncan cut in. "If the humans find out about this, they'll blame us. It wasn't just a Sluagh that killed these men. It was a fae, one we let escape."

"We'd need Kyle on board to fake a call to these men. Something that would have taken them away from the House. Otherwise, the cops will know that they went missing from here," Tiarnan added.

I blinked at all of them, horror churning through my gut. "You guys can't honestly be saying what I think you're saying."

Balor closed his eye, sucked a deep breath in through his nose, and turned away. "Take care of the situation. Do whatever you think is necessary to keep my people safe."

20

I followed Balor back into the lobby, leaving behind the others. I didn't want to see whatever it was they were about to do, nor did I want to know anything about it. My stomach felt sick, and my palms had gone sweaty. Ever since joining the Court, I'd felt as though I'd belonged to something good, something better than what I'd had when I was alone. These fae were trying to do the right thing. They'd done their best to change this city for good. But this…

I did not like this.

"Balor, wait." I called after him. He slowed to a stop, but he didn't turn to face me.

"What is it, Clark?"

"Come on, you don't really think we should cover up their deaths, do you? They'll have families, people who love them. They deserve to know the truth about what happened to them."

His sigh sounded like a rustling paper in the wind.

"Not when the truth is too terrible for them to

know," he said, turning slowly to face me. "Right now, humans know about us, about vampires, about shifters. That alone has been difficult enough for them to face. The Sluaghs have been dormant long enough that they didn't need to know about them, too. The undead are a part of our reality that would terrify them. Do you truly think things would go well—for us or for them—if they found out the truth?"

"No, I don't. But there has to be some other way. Letting them find out about Sluaghs would be bad for us all, but this is bad, too, Balor."

His indifferent, hard, stone cold mask dropped away, revealing the world-weary fae beneath. "Welcome to life in the Crimson Court. Welcome to leading a Court, of protecting two hundred London fae, plus far more scattered throughout Europe. As much as I care for the humans of the city, far more than you'll ever understand, my fae must come first. They always have, and they always will."

He spun on his feet and disappeared.

~

I was leaning back in one of the swivel chairs while Kyle read out case details—a report about a wild-haired ghost haunting a pub—when Tiarnan came back from his abhorrent mission. He didn't look any worse for wear, neither physically or mentally. He seemed quite chirpy, really. I guessed disposing of bodies didn't really shake a centuries-old fae warrior. Maybe he'd done this very thing a hundred times before.

I hoped I never got to the point where I was that immune to the horrors of this world.

I lifted my new, clean boots off the table and grounded them on the floor when he came striding over to me with an uneasy sense of purpose on his boyish features. Ugh. What did he want now?

Arching a brow, I crossed my arms over my chest. "If you've got a problem with your dead body situation, I'm not helping you. That's your thing. Not mine."

"No, that's taken care of," he waved, almost dismissively. "You and I have a new mission."

"I'm not really feeling a mission with you right now, Tiarnan. Not after what you've just been involved with. Like I said, I want nothing to do with it." I waved at Kyle, who had hunched further over his computer when Tiarnan entered the room, like he was bracing himself for the argument he knew was coming. "Besides, I'm helping Kyle. We are thirty reports into a pile of three hundred, so we'll be busy for awhile."

"Kyle doesn't need your help. And anyway, this is Balor's order."

I sat a little straighter in my chair.

"Yeah, I thought that might get your attention." He sighed. "He wants us to visit Caer to see if she has any insight into what is going on here. It's his last resort. To be honest, I'm surprised he requested it."

"Why is Caer his last resort and why does it have to be you and me?" I realised that second bit came out a little harsh, but I was weirded out by his suggestion to cover up what had happened to the cops. I mean, I was no expert on honour, but that didn't seem particularly honourable to me. I actually understood far more why Balor had agreed to it than I understood why Tiarnan had suggested it in the first place.

It seemed like the total opposite of something a Fianna would do, which made me wonder what else I'd gotten wrong when it came to this fae.

"Caer doesn't always provide helpful prophecies when asked. She is testy. The more you ask of her, the further into insanity she dips. We try to save the questions for when things get really tough."

Sighing, I leaned forward, elbows on knees. "Like now."

"Like now."

"And why you and me?"

"He insisted it be you. He seems to think you'll have better odds of extracting something useful from her." He lifted his shoulder in a shrug. "As for me, I volunteered. Balor refuses to go himself. He doesn't like it when she reads him. So, it has to be someone else. I've been there before, so I know the way. Might as well be me."

I shivered at his words. As a new member of the House, I'd only met Caer once. At my trial and induction into the Court. She'd been unnerving, to say the least. She'd gotten into my head, and I'd sworn she'd seen my past. And, what was even worse than that, I was pretty certain she'd placed me with Balor knowing he would flip the fuck out if he knew where I'd come from.

So, I wasn't really into the idea of her reading me again either.

I leaned back in my chair again, crossed my arms. "Nah, I'll pass."

A strange dark magic swirled over my body, rustling at my hair and pulling at my skin. It curled around my center, snapping so tight it almost knocked the breath out of my lungs.

Ouch.

"Trying to say no to a Master's order doesn't feel great, does it?" Tiarnan asked dryly.

Kyle's tapping finally stopped, and he shot me a quick glance through his mop of curly red hair. "Oh yeah. Don't do that, Clark. It won't end well. You're going to have to go. I'll be fine here by myself."

I bit back the growl that threatened to spill from my throat and glared at Tiarnan. "You sure someone else can't go with me? Like Kyle?"

"Nooooot happening," Kyle said, and then resumed his typing.

Tiarnan's expression was pained, and I hated that it made me feel guilty. I didn't have anything to feel guilty about.

With a sigh, I pushed up from the chair and grabbed the sword I'd propped up against the desk. "Fine. Let's get it over with."

∽

Caer was one of the few fae who lived outside of the confines of the House. She lived in Devon, in a little hut on the edge of The Lake of the Dragon's Mouth. Rumors suggested that the lake was one of the few original sources of magic in the world, which made sense. Caer, a reader of the past and the future, would want to live as close to magical veins as she could.

We took one of the SUVs parked in the hidden exit, though Balor had the car brought out front. Most likely to keep said exit as secret as he could. As I climbed into the car, I couldn't help but inwardly smile at the fact that he'd let me in on his secret escape hatch but kept it from Tiarnan.

The four hour drive was long and silent. I didn't have much to say to Tiarnan after his little stunt, and apparently, he didn't have much to say to me either. I hated that things were tense between us now when at one point they had felt so easy. But I couldn't ignore what he had done, and the whole thing made me feel uneasy about him.

Finally, the harsh tension broke when Tiarnan pulled the car to the side of the road in what felt like the middle of blooming nowhere. We were halfway up a mountain, and tall trees swayed in the wind. Rain pelted down from black skies above. Good thing we'd brought our wellies.

"Now what?" I asked, staring out the windshield at the pelting rain.

"We need to go the rest of the way by foot," he said. "The lake is in the center of this mountain. We'll need to go over the peak to get down into the center of it."

"So, it's like a volcano."

He chuckled. "Minus the lava part, but yes."

"Brilliant."

Together, we stepped out into the pouring rain. My poncho rippled in the strong wind, and the plastic hood did little to keep the cold pellets from biting at my skin. My wellies sloshed through the standing water as we moved off the pavement and onto grass. It took me back to that moment in the catacombs, when I'd straddled Balor, and he'd looked at me like he'd never seen anyone more beautiful in his life.

Too bad I was really bad at reading people's expressions. He obviously hadn't been thinking that at all.

The climb up the hill felt like it took as long as the car journey. We sloshed and slipped, grasping onto wet branches. The trees were thick all around us, helping to shield some of the rain. Still, everything was soaked through. When we finally reached the apex, I stared down below us at the valley between the peaks.

And I gasped.

The curtain of rain came to a sudden stop, forming a perfect circle around the valley. Brilliant green grass bloomed all across the hills, along with flowers of every shade imaginable. Silver and bright blue, orange that glowed gold, and purple in a shade so vivid that it almost hurt my eyes.

In the very center of it all sat a lake. No, it was *more* than just a lake. It was a glowing orb of rippling water that was so blue that it looked like a clear sky at twilight. Tiny silver stars even dotted the surface. Fish, I realised, when they began to dart through the light current. More flowers bloomed along the edge of it, long branches curving over the water.

At the very edge of the lake, beside a cluster of smooth stones, sat a hut made of grass. It only had four walls. No roof. From this angle, I couldn't see inside, but I imagined Caer sitting on a small wooden chair, her eyes vacant as she searched the magic for the truth about what was to come.

Suddenly, I felt very insignificant. Confronted with

this kind of power, this kind of magic, I was very small. A tiny speck in the grand scheme of things. My actions might cause ripples, but they would never cause a flood.

"Beautiful, eh?" Tiarnan smiled when I dragged my eyes away from the breathtaking scene before me. "I remember the first time I visited the Lake of the Dragon Mouth. I imagine I had an expression much like yours."

"Why is it called the Lake of the Dragon Mouth?" I asked, realising I probably should have asked that question a hell of a lot sooner than this. I'd never heard of dragons actually existing in this world, but I was quickly realising that there was a lot I didn't know about the supernatural.

"Not because of actual dragons if that's what you're asking." He winked. "*Dragon* is a metaphor for magic. Some say that this place is the mouth to the other world, where magic originated. If you swim deep enough in these waters, you'll find yourself in the realm that created us all. According to legends, anyway. Many have tried to swim back, but they never make it."

Shivers coursed along my skin as I turned my gaze back toward the lake. We, the fae, had been living with humans for so long that there were only a few stories of there ever being a time and a place that was not this. Many believed that we had always been here, that we'd evolved alongside humans. Others felt we'd come from somewhere else. But there was no proof. Only whispers of stories that had been transformed over the years.

A dark figure appeared through the open doorway of the hut, and her gaze turned skyward, toward us.

"Ah." Tiarnan's smile died. "Caer knows we're here. We better start moving down, or she'll think we're intruders. And that is the last thing we want. Trust me."

21

It took us another half hour to get down the side of the mountain. Caer stood waiting for us in the lush valley, her long dark hair whispering across her shoulders in the gentle breeze. The temperature had warmed considerably as we'd descended. No longer did it feel like we were in the middle of London's wet and chilly winter but on an island in the middle of the Mediterranean Sea.

I pulled my poncho over my head as we made our final descent, basking in the rare sun shining down on our heads. The warmth was soothing, but there was no denying that there was something strange about it. It almost seemed fake, like it was hiding something much darker and colder underneath it. Like an icy chill would suddenly show itself if we so much breathed in the wrong direction. Magic rippled across every surface of this place, a bass drum throbbing with every step we made. It grew stronger as we approached the lake.

Caer's dark eyes were hollow as she stared at us.

Two black orbs in a pale face mostly hidden from view by her long hair. "Tiarnan and Clark. I saw you coming."

"Erm, great," I said as chirpily as I could, even though the whole thing made me uneasy. If she could see that we'd been on our way, what else was she able to see? No wonder Balor didn't want to come. "Then, you know why we're here?"

"The gift first," she said in a monotone voice.

"The gift?" Um, were we supposed to bring her a gift? I had missed that memo.

"Here you are, Caer." Tiarnan pulled a small brown object from beneath his poncho and pressed it into Caer's bone-like fingers. She greedily clutched it to her chest, nodded, and then slid it into the pocket of her long gown.

"What was that?" I asked.

"No matter," Tiarnan said.

I frowned, but Caer had already begun to turn away and glide-walk down the path away from us. I decided whatever was in that package would have to be a conversation for another time. For now, we needed to find out if Caer could see anything useful about our current issues. I had a sinking feeling that it was going to be a hell of a lot harder than it sounded.

Instead of leading us into her house, Caer drifted toward a cluster of rocks that sat on the edge of the glowing pool of water. She motioned for us to join her, and then she eased down to sit on the largest rock. Her feet dangled out beneath her, her bare toes skimming the blue water. Suddenly, she looked very young. Clear skin, bright eyes, glistening dark hair.

"Sit. Tell me what it is you need to know."

"You're the goddess," I replied. "Shouldn't you have a pretty good idea why we're here?"

Her glittering eyes shot my way. "I know that you wish for many things, Clark Cavanaugh. Shall I speak some of them aloud? I can guarantee that you wish for me to keep them to myself."

My cheeks flamed. I wet my lips and glanced away. "Sorry. I guess I'm just new to this whole prophecy thing."

"Clark is just a little on edge, Caer," Tiarnan said gently. "Things have been difficult at the Court these past few weeks. That's what we've come here to speak with you about."

"I see," Caer said quietly. "I can feel that particular need coming from *you*, Tiarnan, the need to protect the Court as a whole above all else, even above your own honour. But there is a greater need coming from Clark."

I frowned. "What are you talking about? I came here to find out how to save our Court."

"Yesssssss." Caer's toes whipped across the surface of the water even faster. "But that is not the only thing you want to know. Now, is it, Clark? I see a single-eyed fae in your life. One who is known for smiting his enemies. One who is known for hating the world. One who hates everything. Except for maybe you."

My entire body went hot, and I jumped to my feet. "Okay, that's enough. That's not why I've come here, and you know it."

"Sit." Her voice went dark, razor sharp, and so low that she no longer sounded like Caer at all. It was as if another force had taken over her body, and it wanted nothing more than to cause me fear. "I will not give you the information you need to save your Court unless you listen to me."

I wet my lips and stared down at the goddess. I couldn't do this. I couldn't listen to her talk about Balor. I couldn't risk her digging deeper inside of my head. I wouldn't be able to handle that if I were here by myself, but I certainly couldn't do that in front of Tiarnan. What if he heard things that I could never let anyone know? Tiarnan hated shifters, but he would hate me even more if he knew the truth.

Wincing, he glanced up at me. "Sorry, Clark. I don't really want to hear her talk about your feelings for Balor any more than you do, but we don't have much of a choice. You're going to have to sit and listen to what she wants to say. Otherwise, she'll never tell us anything we need to know."

Damn him. Damn Caer. And damn Balor Beimnech. He was what this whole thing was about. He was why she wanted to read me. If it wasn't for his stupid hold over me, we'd be well on our way to hearing what we had to do in order to save the Court.

Slowly, I eased myself back down on the rock, but I kept myself poised to run if she said too much. "Fine."

Caer turned toward me slowly, her dark eyes turning an even deeper shade of black. "You wish to know why he pushes you away, even as he draws you close."

I swallowed hard and kept my gaze firmly locked on her face. I could imagine what Tiarnan was thinking now. Something smug, about knowing there was something between me and Balor all along. Not that it mattered now.

"Confirm," Caer said, her voice going sharp.

A shiver slipped down my spine. "Yeah, okay. You're right. I want to know why Balor is so back and forth all the damn time. He keeps saying there's a reason he pushes me away, but he won't say what it is. There. I admitted it. Are you happy?"

A ghost of a smile flickered across her face. "The first step toward surviving the future is accepting the past."

Blood pounded in my ears, and I found my fingernails digging into the rock. Were we still talking about Balor? Or had she turned her attention to something else?

"Caer," I said in a rough voice. "Please."

Out of the corner of my eye, I could see Tiarnan furrow his eyebrows.

Caer's eyes went white. "Twenty years ago, Balor came to me for help much like you have today. Unfortunately, I could not see what he wanted me to see. Instead, I saw something else."

I found myself leaning forward, nails bending against the force of my grip on the stone. "What did you see?"

"I told Balor how he will die."

Breath slipped out of my parted mouth.

I wasn't sure how much time passed by. Caer stared at me, and I stared at Caer. Tiarnan was staring at both of us, clearly just as intrigued as me. But I wasn't sure I wanted to hear any more of this. Deep down inside, Caer could see that I wanted to know why Balor kept himself away from me, but the very last thing I wanted to hear was anything about his death.

That meant it must be linked. A thought that terrified me.

In fact, the idea that he would die at all shook me to my very core. He was Balor the smiter. The powerful Prince with an eye that could burn the entire world to the ground. Nothing could defeat him. So, how could he ever die?

Finally, Caer spoke again, and the horrible words I didn't want to hear came storming into my mind. "One day, Balor the great smiter will have a son. Laughter and love will fill his life. When that son is grown, he will kill the Prince of the Crimson Court. And then the Court will be torn to shreds by all of his enemies."

The rock beneath me felt as though it had tipped to the side.

"No," I whispered. "No, that can't be right."

"So, now you have your answer," Caer said, in a much chirpier tone than was warranted for this horrible conversation. "Balor will not mate with you because he is afraid that you will bear him a son. The son that will one day turn his dagger on his own father."

"You're wrong," I said, shaking my head. "There's no way that can be true. Balor has sex all the time. I mean, that's his whole thing. He sleeps with a new girl every Saturday night. Everyone knows about it. He flaunts it. He—"

"It's a lie," Tiarnan said quietly. "It's something I've suspected for a long time. No one has ever actually seen him with someone. There is a lot of flirting and flaunting in that glass box at his club, but there's never been evidence there's anything more. I've always wondered why…heirs are important. Now I understand."

I shook my head. No. It couldn't be. I'd had my own doubts about his promiscuous ways. Hell, I'd even *hoped* he was pretending to sleep with all those girls. But not like this. Not because of this. Balor's own son…

No wonder he pushed me away. No wonder he wouldn't let anyone get close to him. He had been told his own kin would kill him. His own flesh and blood. He'd had to lock away his heart, fully knowing that he could never give it away. The second he did, he would sign his own death warrant.

I stared at the rippling water for a very long time.

"Why does he pretend?" I finally asked. "What's the point of it?"

Caer sniffed. "If I were to guess, it is because he does not want his enemies to know his weakness. Nor would he want them to know he'll never have an heir. Or, if he does have an heir, he will end up killing him. So, he pretends that he is not looking for love."

I glanced up sharply then, stared at Tiarnan. "Not a word of this to anyone else. Do not tell Fionn."

He gave a solemn nod, placed his hand on his chest. "I will do the honourable thing."

I stared at him for a long moment before nodding. "Fine. Okay."

He turned to the goddess. "Caer, we have now listened to what you wanted to say. Is there any chance you could help us with the situation at Court."

She let out a sigh. "Very well. What is it you would like to know?"

"There is a sorcerer creating an army of Sluaghs

as a way to take down the Court. He's changing vampires, shifters, and fae, too. We need to know who he is, and we need to know how we can stop him."

"The Army of the Dead is coming," Caer intoned.

Tiarnan frowned. "Yes, which is why we need to stop it."

She blinked her eyes, as if she were clearing away a particularly nasty vision from her mind. "There is a dark prophecy about the dead that will come. An army of Sluaghs who are supernatural in origin. They are stronger, more resilient to the ashen curse, and they are much harder to kill. They will kill many humans, and your Court will suffer as a result."

"Tell us something that we don't know," I said in a flat voice.

She turned to me then, dark eyes glittering with power. "The sorcerer lives among the dead. He is a man who hides behind many faces, some you have already seen. Some have been in your Court. The only way to find him now is to join him in a place full of death."

My heart thumped hard, and I frowned. "Erm, that was…not exactly what I was hoping for, if I'm being honest. What faces? What place of death? Do you mean a cemetery?"

"Of course not," the goddess quipped. "You must *join him in a place full of death.*"

"I don't understand what that means."

"Nor do I," Tiarnan said, frowning. "You were clear about what you meant when it came to Balor's past. Can you be that clear with this? A lot of lives are at stake."

"Only the faces know who the sorcerer is," she

said in an impatient voice. Quickly, she stood and began to walk away from us. No longer was she gliding, but rushing on a pair of wobbly feet. "I am done speaking. You may go now."

Tiarnan and I glanced at each other and began to move after her. Suddenly, the sky darkened and thunder clapped overhead. Caer whipped toward us, her eyes so dark that they looked like twin black moons. Hair churned around her shoulders, the force of her power swirling around her like a hurricane. "I said go now. While I still let you live."

22

"So, that was fun," I said when Tiarnan and I were finally back inside the safety of the car. I'd dropped my poncho on my hasty retreat out of the valley, giving one last glance at the Lake of the Dragon Mouth before rushing through the sheet of rain. The whole lake had transformed from blue to black as we'd scurried away, dark clouds peppering the sky. "Why did she get so pissed off?"

"Like I said, Caer is testy." Tiarnan yanked the drenched poncho over his head and tossed it into the backseat. "And quite mad at times. The tiniest thing can set her off. I imagine she didn't like us not understanding what she meant."

I blew my damp red hair out of my face. "What the hell *did* she mean? I thought she was going on about a cemetery, but clearly that wasn't it."

"I haven't the foggiest," he said, cranking the engine. "But we've got a team of smart fae back at Court, and I'm confident that one of them will be able to figure it out."

"My money's on Kyle."

Tiarnan shifted his gaze my way, grinned. "I think Duncan will surprise you. He seems like he's all brute strength, but I think he's hiding something more behind the beefy muscles."

"Sounds like you have a crush."

"Everyone has a crush on Duncan."

"You're just saying that because he helped you get rid of the bodies."

His smile died. "Clark, come on. Look, what we did isn't something that I'm proud of, but we didn't have a lot of time to make a decision. Half an hour later, and the path would have been full of humans. It was all or nothing. I chose all."

Sighing, I turned away. "I don't want to argue about it. I know you were trying to do the right thing. I just…guess I disagree that it was the right thing."

"What was the right thing then? Telling the human authorities and letting the cat out of the bag about the Sluaghs?"

I dropped my forehead against the cool window, stared out at the pouring rain. "I don't know."

"You know what? Me either. So, we did what we had to do."

~

Luckily, there hadn't been any more emergencies at the Court while we'd been gone on our prophecy-hunting mission. Everything looked surprisingly normal as we strode up the front steps, down the hall, and into the command station. No more fae Sluaghs. No more dead bodies. And no more explosions.

That said, I was pretty sure it would only be a matter of time.

Kyle glanced up when we strode inside. He was still knee-deep in paperwork, I presumed. "Ah. Good. You're back."

I glanced around. "Where's Balor? We have an update from Caer."

"In his penthouse. He asked me to send you up when you got back."

His penthouse? Damn. I wasn't entirely sure I was ready to see him, not after the mother-load of info that Caer had dropped on me, but I *definitely* knew that I wasn't ready to be inside of his penthouse.

Tiarnan gave a nod. "Don't worry. I'll be right there with you."

"No, sorry," Kyle interjected as we turned to go. "He wants Clark to go on up by herself."

"By myself, but—" I furrowed my eyebrows. I didn't want to go by myself. I didn't want to look into Balor's red eye, knowing the truth about both his past and his future. "We both went on the prophecy-hunting mission."

Kyle guzzled a soda can, seemingly in one long gulp. When he was done, he wiped his lips with the back of his arm. "Look, I don't make the rules. If I did, we'd have a massive game night every time the seasons change instead of those balls. Balor wants you to go up there alone."

Grimacing, I turned toward the door. "Sorry, Tiarnan."

"No worries. Just fill me in when you're done."

I took slow steps up toward Balor's penthouse. I'd only been here twice before. The first time I'd been spying on him, hoping to find out if he was the serial killer taking out London's fae. Thinking back on that now, it had been such a ridiculous assumption. Balor Beimnech was a lot of things, but a serial killer he was not, especially a killer of his own fae. I had quickly learned that the Prince would rather tear apart the entire world than see even a single fae hurt.

The second time I'd been in his penthouse, I'd woken up in his bed after collapsing in front of the entire Court, trying to read every single mind in the room. It had been too much for me to take, and I'd passed out from the toll of it. And then promptly found myself in his bed. We'd kissed, and then he'd pushed me away. It had been one of the *many* times we'd done that song and dance. Now, I understood why.

With a deep breath, I raised my fist to knock. The door swung open wide before my knuckles made contact. I froze, hand held in the air. Balor stood just inside his penthouse, his hair disheveled, his shirt rumpled.

He met my gaze, and my hand drifted to my side. I opened my mouth to speak, but no words came out.

"Did she tell you?"

I wasn't entirely sure which prophecy he meant. The one I'd gone to get from her about the sorcerer or the one about him. Surely he must have known there was a chance I'd find out. That was probably why he'd refused to go himself.

Instead of answering, I gave a nod.

"Good." He opened the door wider and gestured for me to come inside. "Come in, and let's talk things through."

I eased into his penthouse. In the daylight, it was just as magnificent as it was at night. A chandelier hung down, sparkling with a million different crystals. The far window was one large sheet of glass, looking out onto the city's glittering landscape. Buildings dotted the bank of the river, and boats drifted by lazily. His bed, covered in silk sheets, stood tall and commanding in the corner of the room. He gestured to a leather sofa, but then he frowned.

"You're wet."

"Um, yes. It was a Devon mountain in winter. We ran into some rain."

"Stay here." Balor disappeared through a door and reappeared with a black t-shirt and a thick pair of socks. After he handed them to me, he turned to give me privacy, like he hadn't already seen me half-naked before. Still, I was grateful for the small act. After what I'd heard from Caer, I wasn't in the mood to throw myself at him. For once. Not when I knew what the result would be. He would never give in, and I didn't blame him. It could be the beginning of his end.

I wouldn't even want him to give in now. The risk was far too great.

"Okay, I'm decent now," I said after I'd pulled the shirt over my head. As he turned around, I sank into the sofa and pulled the socks over my chilled feet.

They were warm and woollen, soothing after the long day I'd spent trekking around in the mountains.

I was glad to be back in the city.

But I wasn't glad about the discussion we were about to have.

Balor took the armchair across from me, steepled his fingers under his chin, and eyed me warily. "Your tone of voice is different. And you are looking at me differently than you normally do. You even smell different. I take it you aren't happy with what Caer told you."

I sucked in a deep breath and plowed forward. "Caer told me two prophecies. She refused to tell me anything about the sorcerer until I listened to something else she had to say."

His eye went dark. "And what was this something else?"

My mouth went dry, and my skin buzzed with electricity. I could feel his magic pulsing off him in waves, the tension in his body so tight that he probably didn't even realise he was doing it.

"An older prophecy," I said in a soft voice. "One she's told to you."

Balor's eye slipped shut, and his fingers tightened into fists. He leaned back in his chair, taking deep breaths in and out of his nose. All I could do was watch him. I couldn't imagine how he felt. Caer had not only told me his worst and deepest fear but his darkest secret as well. I would have been horrified if I'd been in his place.

"She should not have told you," he said in a low growl, eyes still shut tight.

"I agree. It's not her story to share with whomever

she pleases. Still, she made us listen. Tiarnan heard it, too."

"I suppose you have questions."

I pulled my legs onto the sofa and curled them beneath me, sinking deeper into the soft material. "No. What she said was enough. I don't want to make you talk about it."

His eye flipped open. "Aren't you curious? Aren't you angry? I sleep with other women, and I—"

"No, you don't, Balor."

"There's such a thing as protection these days. Condoms and pills and—"

"I know you. Those things don't work one-hundred percent of the time. You would find that too great of a risk."

He ground his teeth together, clearly not getting the reaction from me that he wanted. What did he expect? For me to be angry? This prophecy wasn't his fault. He hadn't done this to himself. And, in truth, it had nothing to do with me. Yes, it meant I could never be with him the way I wanted, but this wasn't about me. It was about him. He'd had to live for so long with this knowledge, and he'd continue to live with it for many years to come. He'd cut himself off from everyone around him, too afraid to let down his walls.

I felt *bad* for him.

"I never wanted you to know about this," he finally said. "It's best if no one knows at all. This is a burden I carry for myself."

Tears pricked the corners of my eyes. "I know, and I understand why. It's dangerous information for the wrong person to have. But you can trust me. I would never reveal this to anyone. You have to know that."

"That's not why I kept it from you, Clark. I—" He shut his eye again. "There was a part of me that wanted you to keep wanting me, to keep thinking that maybe I was just being a muppet. Now that you know the truth, everything between us will change. I can already see the pity on your face. That's not the way I want you to look at me."

I stood and crossed the room, sinking onto my knees before him. I took his strong hand in mine and squeezed tight. "You're right. I feel bad for you, but not in the way you think. You've had to carry this burden alone for so long, and you shouldn't have to do that. You feel like you've had to construct so many walls between yourself and the world. Keep everyone out. Keep your heart trapped within. For awhile, I *did* think it was because you were just a muppet, if I'm honest. But as much as I hate this damn prophecy, I'm glad you're not. And I'm glad that I know you're not."

"Oh, Clark." His voice was rough as he wrapped his hand around mine. We held on tight to each other, our gazes locked. "Your heart is so big, so human. Maybe it's for the best that you found out, because now you truly understand why we can never take things further."

My heart pulsed in my chest. "You know, not everything has to be about sex, Balor. There are other things that we can share…" Other things that we could do.

Balor sucked in a shuddering breath and slowly pulled his hand out of mine. "I wish it were that easy, Clark. But I know myself. If I got too close to you, if I let myself feel you the way I want to feel you, I don't know that I would be able to hold myself back."

It took all my self-control not to climb onto his lap and wrap my body around his once again. Truthfully, I wasn't sure I would be able to control myself either. I wanted him so badly, it blocked out all my other thoughts. His allure was too strong for me to resist. Maybe he felt the same.

He cleared his throat. "You said two prophecies. Tell me what she said about the sorcerer."

Slowly, I stood, grateful for the change of subject. If we kept talking about our desires, I wasn't sure how much longer I would have been able to resist. Instead, I had something else to focus on. The bloody prophecy, and Caer's nonsensical words. I filled Balor in, being careful to phrase her statements as accurately as I could. When I finished, his scowl reflected my reaction to her words.

"It sounds like there's nothing we can do," he said. "It sounds like we have to prepare."

"Prepare for what?"

"The Army of the Dead."

23

Tiarnan was leaning against the doorframe when I returned to my room, my nose clogged from the sniffles I'd let out on the way back from the penthouse. I didn't want to be an idiot, but I couldn't help my disappointment. The way Balor made me feel was unlike anything I'd ever experienced in my life. And he'd been right. A part of me had hoped, deep down inside, that he would one day realise he was being an idiot, sweep me off my feet, and carry me to his bed.

But I'd been very, very wrong.

We were not meant to be together. We would never get to explore the full depth of how we felt. And I didn't know how anyone else would ever compare to him.

"So, I assume you and Balor had that chat?"

If Tiarnan noticed the redness in my eyes, he did not comment on it. "Yeah, I told him about both of the prophecies. He isn't pleased. Not that we expected anything else."

"You don't look particularly happy yourself." He shifted out of the way when I dug my key into the lock and pushed open the door. "You alright?"

He trailed in behind me. I tossed my wet shirt and socks onto the hamper and plopped straight back onto the bed. "I'll be fine. It's just been a draining day. You know, the whole insane prophecy lady and all."

He quirked a smile. "Was that really today? Feels like a year ago."

"Tell me about it," I mumbled.

"Anything I can do to cheer you up?"

I looked up at him, thinking about Balor's words. We needed to prepare for the Army of the Dead now, which meant I needed to train and I needed to come to grips with my power.

"Actually, I think I could use that name now, for your shifter friend."

Tiarnan's eyes lit up. "I knew you'd change your mind."

I handed him a notepad I kept on my bedside table. He scribbled the name and put the pad back in its place, and then perched on the bed beside me. "How was Balor, anyway? About the whole…"

He didn't elaborate, and he didn't need to.

"He wasn't upset with me, if that's what you're asking. Caer, on the other hand, will probably get a stern talking to next time he sees her."

"I doubt Caer bows to anyone, not even the great Balor Beimnech."

I had to laugh at that, even if it sounded hollow. Not because it was particularly funny but because the tension of the day had really worn me thin. This world was bonkers. Absolutely one-hundred percent blooming mad. I'd thought I had a handle on things when we defeated Lesley, but that had only been the beginning of the most intense weeks of my life.

And something told me things were only going to get worse.

Tiarnan shifted closer, his coal black hair falling across his forehead, and braced a hand on the headboard. The laughter died on my lips as I stared into his dark eyes. His gaze softened, and he gave me a little smile. Something within me drew me closer to him. I was feeling lost, confused, and more than a little emotional. Tiarnan, even though he had recently proven himself to be less than perfect, had been nothing but nice to me. He'd tried to get to know me, time and time again. Oh, and he didn't carry a prophecy around with him that meant he could never have sex again, for fear of creating the very thing that would one day kill him and destroy his entire Court.

It would be so easy to give in to the desire I saw in his eyes. It would be so easy to lean forward and kiss him. And I wanted to, in a way. The tension in my body begged for release. I wanted to feel someone's hand on my skin, feel someone's lips on mine. All I had to do was lean forward and—

I sucked in a sharp breath and pulled back.

Tiarnan frowned.

My face burned. "I'm sorry. I can't."

With a sigh, he stood. "Balor had a reason for pushing you away. What's your reason for pushing me away?"

"Balor."

Tiarnan actually laughed. "This is a mistake, Clark. You can never be with him."

"Maybe so," I said quietly. "But I'm not going to throw myself at someone just because I can't have who I want."

"Ouch." He pressed a hand against his heart and stepped backward. "I'll leave you to it then. It's a shame, really. I thought things could be different between you and me, now that you knew the truth about him, but…I was wrong."

～

An hour later, I had showered, dried my eyes, and changed into a fresh set of guard clothes. Balor had called the entire Court into the Throne Room for an announcement. The guard team stood by his side, half of us on one end and half on the other. Fae spread out through the large domed hall, staring up at us with varying degrees of confusion, hope, and fear plastered across their faces.

I stared out at them, now fully understanding what Balor meant when he said he would do anything to protect them. They knew he would do anything for them, and the trust in their eyes was unparalleled to anything I'd ever seen in my life. They put their lives in his hands, and he repaid that trust in spades.

They would probably never know just how much he sacrificed to keep them safe.

He wouldn't even want them to know. He wouldn't want them to worry.

He just wanted them to live their lives in peace.

"Welcome, everyone. I'm sorry I've had to call this meeting under such difficult circumstances once again. I can promise that our next Throne Room meeting will be of a much happier nature." He gave a slight smile. "Once this current situation has been taken care of, we'll begin our preparations for the Spring Ball."

Oh, god. Inwardly, I rolled my eyes. I was not looking forward to this Spring Ball, but I understood why Balor brought it up. He wanted to give them something to look forward to, and to provide the illusion that everything was just fine. If a ball was coming? Nothing to worry about, right?

Excited murmurs echoed through the lofted space. Balor held up a hand, and everyone quietened. "Unfortunately, we do have a serious issue to take care of first, as I am sure you are all aware. A sorcerer has decided that this Court, this House, is his target. He would like to see the Crimson Court fall into ruin. We cannot let that happen."

More murmurs drifted through the crowd.

"He has attacked us several times, and he plans to do so again. Next time, he will bring a group of Sluaghs with him."

I couldn't help but notice that he used the word *group* instead of army. Smart move. If he simply threw out the words 'Army of the Dead', chaos would ensue.

"Our guard team works diligently to keep this House safe," Balor said, gesturing toward us from his throne of crimson skulls. "However, we do not know how many Sluaghs the sorcerer will bring with him. We may need more fighters, and I know we have some strong ones here. Would any of you like to volunteer to help us in our fight against the dead?"

Dozens of hands shot up into the air. At least thirty. Maybe even more. My heart lifted at the strength and determination I saw on the fae faces. We might not have been able to stop the sorcerer from bringing his army here, but he would not be able to destroy us.

I turned toward Balor with a smile, but it was short-lived. The ground beneath my feet began to shake, and a boom ripped through the Throne Room.

24

I was by Balor's side in an instant, shielding his body from view of our attackers. The fae had begun to scream. They were running through the room, darting this way and that, making it impossible to see exactly what we were dealing with.

The sorcerer. It had to be. We'd come together to prepare for his attack, but he'd arrived with his undead army far sooner than we'd expected.

Several of the fae who had volunteered for the fight rushed up the stairs. They joined us on the stone platform where Balor's throne sat high above the crowd, their bodies tense, ready to fight. They were fae of all ages, all sexes, and all sizes. We all locked gazes, our expressions grim, and then we turned toward the open doors of the Throne Room.

Balor stood behind us. Even with the dozens of fae now standing in a protective circle around him, he radiated with more power than all of us combined. He stood tall, hands curling into fists.

"Elise. Cormac. Calm everyone down and get

them to safety." He pushed through his crowd of protectors, drew his sword, and strode down the stone steps, his dark coat billowing behind him. "Everyone else. Come with me."

Another boom shuddered through the building, but it did nothing to slow Balor down. He just kept striding toward the open door, his back straight, his head lifted high. I drew my own sword and hurried after him. Everyone around me did the same.

When we reached the lobby of the building, everything suddenly became brutally clear. Fionn stood out on the front lawn with his back toward the river. He smiled broadly when we stepped out onto the front veranda, and then gestured at the dozen or so humans that surrounded him. Some were cops, some were reporters, others were witnesses who must have wandered in on curiosity alone.

I kind of wanted to punch him in the face.

"Fionn." Balor's voice boomed as he stared down at his fellow Master, one who should answer to Balor and Balor alone. Instead, he was here, launching an all-out attack on his own Court.

"Balor." Fionn smiled and then glanced at me. "I see you still have your trusty mind-reader doing your every bidding. Like, killing human cops and then hiding the bodies?"

I sucked a sharp breath in through my nose, and the world seemed to slow around me. Fear churned through my gut as I stared at Fionn. I understood what he was doing now. I knew exactly why he'd brought the cops. I turned to look behind me at the Courtly building that had come to feel like my home. There was no damage to those majestic brick walls.

Nothing to suggest there'd actually been an explosion at all.

Somehow, Fionn, or one of his trusty sidekicks, had tricked us into hearing things that weren't really there.

Magic.

The click of camera shutters filled the night air.

I whirled on my feet, glaring at Fionn. "There were no real explosions, were there?"

"Not this time, I'm afraid." He spread his arms wide, glanced at the cops. "These lovely human authorities asked me for some help. They were afraid to go through your front doors. I can't imagine why. So, they needed a way to draw you out of your House. That way, we have plenty of witnesses if you try to commit any more crimes."

"Like burning us," one of the reporters called out.

"Or slicing us to shreds," a large beefy cop said while crossing his arms over his chest. "Our contact has told us about everything you've done. He's got proof, too. He told us where you hid the bodies. And they were right there where he said."

Balor chuckled. "That's interesting. Since I have done no such thing."

"Ah, here he is. Tell us again where the Prince hid the bodies."

Tiarnan stepped out from the shadows and strode across the lawn to join Fionn, the cops, and the humans that surrounded him. Confusion rippled through me. All I could do was stare. What the hell was going on? Tiarnan wasn't some kind of *source*. He'd been working by our sides. He'd been helping us track down the sorcerer.

"Tiarnan?" I asked, my soft voice drifting across the lawn. "What's happening? What's going on?"

He kept his eyes focused on the ground. "Sorry, Clark. This was never about you. I'm sorry you had to get involved."

Blood roared in my head as I stared at him, more shocked than I had ever been in my life. My feet stumbled as I took a step back. A strong hand pressed up against me, to keep me from splatting right onto the ground. Moira. I could sense it was her even without turning around. How, I didn't know, but I could.

"How could you?" I asked, tears filling my eyes. "We welcomed you into our House. We took you in when you had nowhere else to go. All this time, you've been working with us...I..."

"That's not *entirely* true," he said, clearing his throat. "Fionn did not truly kick me out of House Futrail. He sent me here to get information that would discredit Balor as the rightful Prince of the Crimson Court. He made the order, and I had to follow." He stared hard at the ground. "I really am sorry, Clark. I didn't want things to happen like this, but I saw no other way. Even though he made the order, I do agree with him. We cannot ally ourselves with vampires and shifters. You've seen what happens when our lives become entwined with other supernaturals. If Balor can't see that, someone else needs to rule the Court instead."

I shook my head, fully understanding everything. "You were the one who hacked the cameras. Twice. You got Maeve out of the House, got Lesley out, too. You've been pretending to work with us this whole time, but really, you were working against us. Launching attacks on your own damn Court."

All this. All this because of the bloody vampires. All this because of his hatred for shifters. Shifters, like me. Trembling, I curled my hands into fists. My shock had gone to full-on anger now. I wanted nothing more than to rush at Tiarnan, to smack some sense into his stupid, dishonourable brain. He had betrayed us in a way that I could never forgive.

He was dead to me.

"You're no Fianna," I said in a low hiss. Then, I turned toward Balor, placing my hand on his arm. "Let's go back inside. They won't come for us in there."

"No." Balor gently pried my hand off his arm and stepped forward. "I will cooperate with the human authorities. I will admit to the crimes I have been accused of. I helped cover up the deaths of the missing cops. Innocents who deserved much better."

A wicked smile spread across Fionn's face, and he shot me a wink. "Guess I'll get to take control of your Court much sooner than I thought. I really thought Balor Beimnech would be harder to take out of the equation than this."

Balor didn't say a word as the human authorities slowly and cautiously crept up the stairs. Several of the fae began to fight against the cops, but Balor ordered them to stop. Despite how much they wanted to make a scene, the word of their Master was too strong to allow them to do anything other than watch.

That included me.

I was desperate to kick some ass. Even though I'd wanted to go to the cops in the first place, this was something else entirely. It was an ambush. And what was worse, Tiarnan had set it all up.

After the cops put Balor into the back of the car, Fionn and Tiarnan strode up the stairs to join us outside of the Crimson Court.

"I can't believe either of you," I spat, blood boiling through my veins. "He's your Prince. He'd do anything to protect you, and you repay him like this?"

"He would do anything *other* than condemn the vampires and the shifters," Fionn tossed over his shoulder as he strode through the front doors of *our* home, not his.

I trailed after him, my entire body shaking. "*I* am a half-shifter."

"Yes, well. Perhaps you'll serve no place in my Court."

"It's not your damn Court!" My words echoed off the vaulted ceiling. Everyone surrounding us stopped to stare. I whirled toward them, throwing up my hands. "Why isn't anyone doing anything to stop this arsehole?!"

Fionn turned to me then, his eyes glittering. "And you think it's yours? You, Filthy Carrion, have been here less than a month. You think you're owed this place far more than me? I have bled for this Court. I have fought for it with every ounce of my being. A few weeks of silly street fights is nothing compared to the centuries of devotion I have given these fae."

"Yeah, you're all high and noble," I said through clenched teeth. "Pretending that you hate the supes. Meanwhile, you're perfectly happy using them when you see fit."

Fionn frowned and glanced at Tiarnan. "Whatever nonsense is she talking about now?"

"The sorcerer who has been making Sluaghs. I can see why she would think it. Lesley got turned after I broke her out of the dungeon. And Maeve got turned after I met with her and tried to convince her to join us."

"Ah, that." Fionn laughed in my face. "Don't be ridiculous. I haven't had anything to do with that. Don't worry. That will be handled in due time, much quicker now that you have someone capable in charge. Now, stop gawking and get back to work. Or else I'll have you banished into the darkness."

25

"This is absolute shite!" I slammed my fist on the table, the sound reverberating through the cavernous command station. After my little confrontation with Fionn, I'd stormed straight in here to slam my fist against the punching bag as many times as I could. That had gotten old really fast, so I'd turned my rage onto the tables.

Half an hour later, and I still very much wanted to punch something. Preferably Fionn's face.

Moira crossed her arms over her chest. "I agree. It's bullshit. The whole cover-up of the cop deaths was Tiarnan's idea. Balor only agreed to it because he didn't want to make the same mistake Fionn did."

"Oh, I think he made that up." Kyle spun the monitor around. There was a story about vampires killing humans outside of House Futrail's home alright, but vampires had been arrested—by Fionn, in agreement with the humans—and the fae had never even been suspected in the murders.

What a lying, murderous arsehole.

"Surely there's something we can do. Fionn can't just take over the Court whenever he pleases, can he? There's a line of succession, right? Someone else truly in charge?"

Duncan frowned. "He can technically take over, which is why no one has taken up arms against Fionn. When a Prince is out of commission, the nearest Master can take command. If anyone objects, well... traitor and all that. Unless there is an heir or a different successor who has been named."

Everyone glanced around at each other. Balor clearly had some kind of back-up plan for whenever things went wrong. He was a cautious enough fae that he wouldn't leave this kind of thing to chance. Lesley had mentioned it once before. She had said it wasn't Duncan. So, if it wasn't the leader of his guard team, then who was it?

"Ah." Elise raised her hand and cleared her throat. "Here's the part where I come clean about the fact that Balor named me as his official successor about thirty years ago. I wasn't supposed to tell anyone. Sorry."

The entire room turned toward Elise in unison. *Elise*, of all people. It was a match that I found both ridiculously surprising but also obvious as hell. She was smart. She was driven. She might not be as mighty of a warrior as some of the others, but she didn't need to be. She just needed to have a good mind and the kind of loyalty that you could depend on.

And that was our girl.

"Right." Duncan strode forward, braced his hands on the table, and glanced at each of us in turn. "In our minds, Elise is our leader. Do you understand? Balor is not here right now, so we have to look to someone else to help us get through this. And it sure as hell isn't Fionn. That said, let's not make this public knowledge just yet. Let them think we're stewing on it. But in this room, Elise is the boss."

"Oh, right, okay," Elise said when Duncan stepped back and passed the metaphorical baton to one of my closest and dearest friends. "I'm not really sure what to say here. Am I supposed to make a speech or something?"

"Just tell us what to do, boss," Moira said with an encouraging fist-bump against her shoulder.

Elise gave a nod, sucked in a deep breath, and then scanned the room. Her eyes landed on me, and something sparked within them. "Clark. We need Balor back. Or else we're never going to win against the Sluaghs. If Fionn didn't have anything to do with that, then...they're still coming."

She didn't need to tell me that. Balor's power was unrivalled. Fionn had some of his warriors here, and we had a handful of fae who were willing to fight against the undead. And everyone individually had their powers. Some were quite impressive, like Lesley's. Others were practically useless in a battle scenario, like mine. And, lest we forget, the sorcerer was transforming supes. They might be able to access their powers, too.

Balor, on the other hand, could burn their whole army down within five minutes. The only way to stop our Prince from using his power was to trap him inside petrol-soaked catacombs. Or get him to willingly go to Scotland Yard. It took him out of the equation, and that was exactly what the sorcerer needed to win this fight.

"You're not wrong," I said. "But Balor pretty much volunteered himself. Probably because he thought the Court was better off if he didn't fight against the inevitable. Tiarnan obviously set this up. He 'disposed' of the bodies, and then told the cops exactly where he hid them. And then he said it was Balor who did it instead."

"The timing is interesting," Kyle said, speaking up for once. "Fionn said that he isn't involved in the whole sorcerer mess, but he appeared at exactly the right time."

Duncan murmured his agreement. Moira nodded.

"I don't know, guys." I frowned. "Tiarnan is a total shithead, and I pretty much want to claw his eyes out for what he's done. But the whole reason he did it is because he hates supernaturals. Why would he help create them?"

Moira lifted her shoulder in a shrug. "Maybe he didn't know what his boss was up to."

"Yeah, but Fionn hates supes, too. He's made that more than clear."

"Fionn is very much a means to an end kind of fae." Duncan fisted his hands and leaned onto the table. "He probably didn't come up with this idea himself. It might have been someone else, and he's just going along with it, because of the promise of power. Someone else who has already tried once to take this Court down."

My eyes widened in understanding. "You mean Nemain, Princess of the Silver Court." My stomach flipped over itself at just speaking her name out loud.

We'd beaten her once, and she was probably angry. And Faerie as a whole had done nothing to punish her for her crimes. She'd gotten away with her treasonous ways, so she'd decided to come after us again. And this time, she'd upped the game.

"I can actually see how this could have been pitched to him," Elise said with a slow nod. "A sorcerer, putting a curse on all those evil supes he hates so much. Two birds with one stone, so to speak."

"And how does that explain the fae who were turned?" I asked.

Elise and Moira exchanged a glance. "It sounds like they approached Maeve about getting involved in this scheme, and she said no. So, they changed her. Hell, maybe even Maeve came here to warn us. And then Lesley? Well, who knows when it comes to Lesley. I can see how they might think she's a liability. I mean, she did kill a bunch of fae."

"On Nemain's orders," I said.

"So she said. And now she's not alive to testify it."

"Shit," I muttered.

"Exactly," Duncan replied. "This whole thing is utter shite."

A few moments passed by while we all stood in silence, thinking through our limited options. Fionn had effectively taken control of the Court, so whatever we did, it would have to be in secret. In his quest for power, he had created literal monsters. Now, we had to fix his mess before the dead swarmed through this House, as well as through the London streets.

"So, what do we do?"

We all looked toward Elise. Her cheeks were pink, but she held her head high, shoulders thrown back like she owned the damn room. Good for her. Elise had always been the quieter, bubblier one, but there was a strength within her. One that I admired. She didn't need to throw a sword around the air like I did in order to make herself feel powerful. I admired that in her.

"Right. I'm going to have to ask Clark to do something I know she hates doing." She winced and turned to me. "Sorry, Clark. We need to know what's going on in Fionn's mind. Then, we'll have a better idea about what to do next. We need confirmation that he's involved with the sorcerer, and we need to know if the sorcerer has plans. Will he still attack even though Fionn has taken over? These are important questions."

"Okay," I said, without hesitation. "But Fionn knows about my power. He's quite defensive about it. If he knows I'm reading his mind, he'll block me out. It will only work if he doesn't know I'm in the room."

Duncan gave a nod. "We'll set a trap."

"Exactly." I nodded and turned to Elise. "Can we come up with some kind of distraction? Something to keep him occupied while I poke around in his brain? It needs to be something good. Something that really catches him off guard. Otherwise, he might sense that I'm there even if he can't see me."

Elise's eyes lit up, and her sweet smile turned just the slightest bit evil. "Oh, yes. I have the perfect plan."

*E*lise was the queen of glamours. After she transformed my face so that I looked like a completely different fae, she shooed me off to wait for her in the restaurant. On my way, I stopped by my room to change into a different set of clothes. I couldn't very well pull off my non-guard charade if I was donning the all-black, signature style of the team. I also couldn't wear a sparkly dress that made me stand out. Instead, I chose a pair of dark slacks and a nondescript blue blouse.

Then, I waited. I asked for the booth in the back corner where I'd had my date with Tiarnan and kept one eye on the door while I ordered a gin and tonic to soothe my nerves. The last time I'd poked around in Fionn's brain…well, it had not gone well, exactly. He'd known what I was doing, and we'd had a strange, tense stand-off in his mind. He'd also called me a Filthy Carrion.

I didn't really want a repeat of the experience. The guy creeped me out, even more so now that I knew he was helping a sorcerer raise an undead army in the middle of bloody London.

After half an hour, Fionn strode through the front doors of the restaurant with a very pretty, well-coifed Elise on his arm. I sat a little bit straighter in my booth. She wore a slinky red number, and she'd somehow managed to curl her long silver strands in the small moments since I'd last seen her. She'd even donned a full face of makeup, and the dark kohl lining her eyes made the silver pop right out. She looked absolutely gorgeous. Fionn definitely noticed. His gaze followed her every move, his eyes full of hunger.

I let out a low whistle and busied myself with my gin and tonic while Mr. Clicky Heels showed Fionn and Elise to their table. The arsehole even pulled out her chair for her. A bonus point move in a normal circumstance, but the fact he pretended to be a gentleman made me want to throw daggers right at his head.

Alas, I could not. I needed to be nonchalant and unnoticeable. And I also needed to listen in on his thoughts. With a deep breath, I shifted slightly further into the booth, trained my eyes on my drink, and let my mind drift away on the current of magic in the air.

I expected resistance when I reached Fionn's mind, but it didn't come. Elise and her beauty had disarmed him. Slowly, I pushed forward and dipped into the mind of one of the most infamous fae warriors that had ever lived.

Forget dinner. I want to throw her over my shoulder and take her straight to my bed.

Inwardly, I rolled my eyes. *Males.*

Why is she asking about the sorcerer? I don't want to talk about this right now. Fine. She's clearly scared, the poor thing. If I make her feel comforted, then it will probably be easier to get into her pants tonight. Not that she's wearing any. I can tell by the way she's clenching her thighs.

Gritting my teeth, I yanked my mind back into my booth. My god, I wanted to grab my fork and shove it right into Fionn's arm. The last thing I wanted to do was to sit here listening to him think about how much he wanted to shag my friend. It was the only thing on his goddamn mind. Elise probably knew it, too. And it probably made her want to gag. I swore, if he tried anything....

Deep breath again. And into his mind I went.

26

Fionn's mind rushed from one thought to the next. Sucking in a deep breath, I pushed in deeper, past his surface thoughts, and past the irritation and desire. He was unhappy but he still couldn't stop staring at her chest. And he didn't like where the conversation had headed.

The sorcerer isn't going to attack now. Why can't she understand that? It was all a dumb charade just to get Balor stuck behind human bars. Sure, we turned a few fae into Sluaghs, but they deserved it.

Now, this Court is mine. Balor will spend the rest of his miserable life away from here. As soon as Faerie confirms my status as the new Prince, the magic will lock my status in place. And then there will be nothing Balor can do to stop me from ruling.

Hopefully, I can one and done this bird before they ring me back tonight.

Slowly, I pulled out of Fionn's mind and smiled. Don't get me wrong. I was incredibly pissed off. What a dick, right? But at least he wasn't as big of a dick as he pretended to be. The sorcerer wasn't a threat to this Court anymore. Only *Fionn* was.

We had to get Balor back before this lying arsehole took control, permanently.

Suddenly, a form slid into the seat opposite me. Frowning, I looked up to tell whoever it was to go away, but my breath caught in my throat when I saw who it was. It was Tiarnan, his eyes dark and hollow. I hadn't noticed he'd even entered the restaurant. I'd been far too focused on Fionn, his mind, and his bloody sex-crazed thoughts.

"Don't freak out," he said in a low voice. "I know it's you under that glamour. When Elise asked Fionn out on a sudden date, I got suspicious. Thought I might find you here, listening in on things. Your expression gave you away. Plus, I've never seen that face in the Court before."

"Get away from me, Tiarnan. I don't care if your Master has presumably taken control of this Court. I will not hesitate to turn my blade on you."

I moved my hand away from my cool drink and rested it on the jacket beside me, where I'd hidden my sword from view. Never before would I have carried it around this Court for protection, but things had quickly changed. I was glad I'd brought it with me now.

"My beef is not with you." He leaned forward and braced his forearm on the table. "It was always with Balor. I just wanted you to know that."

I snorted. "If you have a problem with Balor, then you have a problem with me, and you know that."

His expression darkened. "Yes, because you're half in love with him."

"That's not even true and you know it."

"I said *half* in love with him," he argued. "The other half feels indebted to him for reasons I don't understand. It's almost as if you think you owe him."

"Well, he changed my life, Tiarnan. I was miserable, broke, friendless, and pretty much helpless until he brought me here. I was hiding from the world." I placed my palms flat on the table and leaned forward to glare into his eyes. "I am none of those things anymore because he showed me a different life."

"He orders you around and risks your life for his own purposes. The vamps and shifters are more important to him than his own Court."

"You don't honestly believe that, do you?" I arched a brow. "Just because he's willing to put the past behind him and move forward? Like Caer said, to survive the future, you have to accept the past. It seems like you and Fionn can't. So, you betrayed us all, based on this crazy notion that other supernaturals are worse than you are. You, who let innocent humans get killed, and then blamed their deaths on someone who would have never laid a single finger on them."

Tiarnan stared at me. "You're angry."

"Of course I'm angry," I hissed, careful not to raise my voice too loud. Fionn was halfway across the restaurant, but that didn't mean he wouldn't hear me if I started shouting at one of his warriors. "You used me. You betrayed me. You ripped this Court apart."

He blinked. "I didn't use you, Clark."

"Yes, you did." I shoved my finger at the table. "Right here in this restaurant. You pretended to invite me on a date so that you could needle me for information about Balor."

"I..." He trailed off, and then pressed his lips together.

I let out a hollow laugh. "See. You can't even deny it."

"I actually was interested in you, Clark. I liked you. Hell, I still do, even though it's clear you have eyes for someone else. I asked you on a date because I wanted to pursue that with you."

"You kept asking me about Balor. Don't think I didn't notice."

He winced. "I figured I might as well try to get information about him from you. For some wild reason, he's let you get closer to him than almost anyone else. But that wasn't why I asked you out in the first place. I wanted to date you. But you made your choice very clear. Balor is the one you want. Always has been, and as far as I can tell, always will. You're still fighting for him now, when doing so could end up getting you killed."

My cheeks flushed with heat, and I leaned forward even more. I could feel the adrenaline pumping through me, blood and magic pounding in my ears. No longer did I care if anyone saw me. No longer did it matter if Fionn looked this way.

"Are you actually *threatening* me?" I shook my head, my eyes flashing. "You know, I actually thought you were the nice guy. The good one. The honourable warrior. Hell, the better choice. I can see now that I have never been more wrong about anything in my life."

I pushed myself up from the table and grabbed my jacket, along with the sword hidden beneath it. He moved to stand, but I bared my teeth, knowing that I might very well look insane. But I didn't care.

"Go on. Try to stop me. Tell your Master. See how that one ends. You've done so much damage as it is. Why not go for some more, huh?"

The challenge bounced through the air between us. Tiarnan froze, pain reflected across his every feature. I could feel several eyes on us now, but no one made a move to break up the fight.

"That's what I thought," I said when he didn't make a move. "See you around, Tiarnan. Or actually, maybe not. I wouldn't be here when Balor Beimnech gets back." I paused. "Oh, and you should know that your Master? He was working with the sorcerer all this time."

~

I threw my jacket around my shoulders and went out the secret entrance to grab a car. Half an hour later, I stood in the lobby of Scotland Yard with my sword on display for everyone to see. The receptionist kept casting me uneasy glances, and I kept shooting her a smile full of teeth. I was done playing the nice and easy sweet fae.

I was out for blood.

"Clark Cavanaugh?" The beefy detective who had escorted Balor away from Court strode up to me, stuck out his palm, and gave my hand a firm shake. Not bad. He seemed a little flustered by my presence, but he was holding his ground. And at least he hadn't acted like I was contagious.

He led me down a fluorescent-lit hallway and escorted me into a boxy room that held a metal table and two folding chairs. It looked like one of those interrogation rooms from television. I would have felt uneasy, but he had no idea what was about to hit him. Poor guy.

He was just doing his job.

"Ah, take a sit." He watched me plop down into the chair. Instead of joining me, he jutted out his hip and perched on the edge of the table, crossing his arms over his beefy chest. "Now, I imagine you're here about your friend. I can assure you that we are taking good care of him and that he's fine."

"I'm sure." I shot him that toothy smile, the one I knew set people on edge. "I am actually here to discuss his release."

"Ah." He ran his hand against his balding head and chuckled. "Release? Well, ah, I am afraid that won't be happening anytime soon, love."

"Clark," I said.

"Excuse me?"

"My name is Clark. Not love."

His face flushed. "Now, Clark. I don't want any trouble here. We're just doing our jobs, and your friend has been accused of a very serious crime. Just because he's a fae doesn't mean we can let him get away with murder. Three murders, to be exact."

"He didn't kill them," I simply said. "And you have zero evidence to prove otherwise."

"We have the testimony of another one of your fae, and he showed me where your friend hid the bodies."

I arched a brow. "And what other evidence have you found? DNA? Fingerprints?"

"Erm."

"See, that's what I thought." I placed my palms flat on the table and reached out toward his mind. It was easy getting inside this human's thoughts. Not only were humans easier to read, but he was flustered. And flustered meant defenceless.

We have to charge him. The city will crucify us if we don't. Running for re-election next year, and oh my god, she's going to kill me. Look at her eyes. They've gone all weird. Is she going to put a spell on me?

"I don't do spells," I said coolly, and then smiled.

The detective jumped off the table and put some space between us. "Now, love. I don't know what voodoo you're doing, but you need to stop right now or I'll call some backup in here to deal with you."

"Who is up for re-election? I don't really follow local politics."

He wiped his arm across his damp forehead and turned toward the door.

"I wouldn't do that if I were you. Clearly, I can read your mind. I know what you're hiding. If you don't do as I say, then I will reveal every single one of your secrets to your…wife."

It was a wild guess, a stab in the dark, but I'd caught the silver ring on his finger. Everyone had secrets. What his was, I didn't know, but I figured whatever it was, he probably didn't want his wife to find out.

Oh god, she knows about Julia. If Alison finds out, she'll leave me for good this time.

Ah, bingo. So, I'd guessed right.

"Julia, right?" I tsked and shook my head. "It really would be a shame if Alison found out."

He clasped his hands together, glanced at the door, and then at the two-way mirror. "Fine. I'll do what you want."

I pushed up from the table and smiled. "Good. I'm glad we understand each other. You'll be releasing Balor Beimnech from custody on lack of evidence. If you manage to find something that sticks, then by all means, try charging him again. But just remember, I'll be watching you."

27

Balor strode down the steps of Scotland Yard, looking not even the teensiest bit worse for wear. He had his jacket slung over one shoulder, and his dark silver-streaked hair rustled in the evening breeze. I pushed off the railing from where I had waited for him outside on the pavement, feeling my heart lurch in my chest.

Even though it had only been a few hours, it felt like I hadn't seen him in years.

His gaze landed on me, and his red eye sparked bright. That was it. I couldn't keep it cool anymore. I rushed halfway up the stairs and met him in the middle. He slowed to a stop, his chest brushing against mine. Everything within me wanted to throw my arms around his neck and pull him close, but I stopped myself just in time.

There was still a wall between us. There always would be.

His lips tipped up in the corners. "Clark, you have no idea how good it is to see your face."

"Right back at you, Master." I grinned.

"How'd you manage it?" he asked, glancing over his shoulder. "They seemed pretty intent on nailing me for this one, sans the evidence."

"I might have blackmailed the lead investigator." When Balor's eyebrows shot up, I held up my hands. "I know. I know. But trust me, he deserved it."

"You went poking around in his mind."

I shrugged. "Figured I'd prove that my mind reading skills are actually an asset for once."

He let out a low chuckle. "I have to admit, I never expected you'd use your powers like this, but I'm not going to complain. Sitting in a jail cell while my Court falls apart was making me go a bit mad."

"Ah." The smile died from my face. "About that. Fionn expects to hear from Faerie tonight to get confirmation that he can take over your Court."

He narrowed his eyes, nostrils flaring. "No wonder he was so eager to invade."

"Yeah, and there's some more. Apparently, the whole sorcerer thing was a charade."

"A charade?" He frowned. "Where did you get all this information?"

"Like I said, I'm finally putting my skills to good use."

"Good." Even though I could tell that he wanted nothing more than to throw his fist right into Fionn's face, he managed a smile, just for me. "Come on then. We're likely to need that sweet little brain of yours again before all of this is over."

Balor wanted to take the driver's seat, which was fine with me. On the way, I filled him in on everything that had happened since he'd been arrested, taking great delight in explaining how I'd metaphorically flipped the bird at Tiarnan in the restaurant.

Balor seemed pretty pleased with it, too, if his smug smile was any indication.

"I should have known not to trust him," Balor finally said as he steered the car into the back entrance of the Court. "Though I'm curious how he managed to get past that initial mind reading you did on him the first day he arrived."

"Yeah, so, before you get angry with me, I just want you to know that I really did trust the guy."

"You didn't read his mind."

I winced. "No. He made me feel like he would never speak to me again if I did."

"And you wanted to speak to him again." He flashed me a look as he parked the car. "Because you were interested in him."

I nibbled on my bottom lip. "Yes and no, Balor. You have to know that while there was some interest there, it wasn't…"

He cut the car engine and turned to face me. "It wasn't what?"

It wasn't like it is with you. But I couldn't say that. It would only make things worse.

"It wasn't, I don't know, *complete*. I guess it was a half-hearted interest. I thought there might be something there, but I wasn't sure. I guess I wanted the chance to find out, and I thought if I invaded his mind, I wouldn't get that chance."

He sighed and ran a hand down his face. "Never disobey an order again, Clark."

Was that…it? No shouting? No alpha growling at my face? No pushing me up against the car and shooting his alluring magic waves across my skin? It was like he'd given up.

And I couldn't stand the thought that he had.

Suddenly, Balor tensed and cocked his head. "Do you hear that?"

I frowned. "Hear what?"

And then I heard it. Through the thick car windows, it was barely audible, but it was definitely there. Screams. Dozens of them. And they were coming from inside the Court.

Balor and I threw open the doors and rushed into the building. We found ourselves in a dark corridor, with no light at all. Not even from the overhead chandeliers that usually lit up the place day and night. Screams echoed through the halls, causing every hair on my arms to stand on end. My heart thumped hard as we began moving toward the sounds. What the hell was going on?

Edging in front of me, Balor took a long sniff of the air. "The sorcerer. He isn't here, but he's sent some of his Sluaghs."

"What? I don't understand. Fionn sounded convinced the sorcerer wouldn't attack."

"Fionn was wrong," Balor said in a low growl. "The sorcerer may have told him that he would not attack, but he was most certainly lying. Fionn thought he was using the sorcerer, but really, the sorcerer was using him."

"Shit," I muttered underneath my breath.

This changed everything. How could we deal with both Fionn *and* an Army of the Dead? We couldn't. There was no way we could protect the Court from both of them.

"Fionn will take advantage of this," I said as Balor kicked open a door and motioned me to follow him down the next corridor. "He's likely hiding out somewhere, waiting for that phone call."

"You're likely right," Balor said.

"Where do you think he'll be? In your office?"

"It does not matter." Balor stopped and turned toward me, taking my cheek in his palm. His eye searched my face, softening just long enough to make my toes curl in my boots. "We have to fight off the Sluaghs. If Fionn takes the Court, then so be it."

Blood rushed into my ears. "There has to be some other way. Maybe if we split up. I could go fight the Sluaghs, and you could go stop Fionn."

I didn't volunteer myself to find Fionn because I knew that nothing I could do or say would stop the traitorous Master from taking that call. It had to be Balor. He had to be the one to reclaim his throne. Not me.

And Balor knew it, too.

Once again, he shook his head. "My eye is far too powerful to be wasted on that fae. I need to use my power on the dead."

Balor turned and strode down the hallway, a new purpose taking control of his gait. I hurried after him, drawing the sword from its sheath. I held on tight, gritting my teeth against the building storm of dark magic that swirled through the halls. It bit at my skin, tossing my hair around my face.

When we reached the lobby, everything was chaos. Duncan and Moira were whirling through the crowd, slashing at Sluaghs that were launching themselves at fae with swords bigger than their bodies. Elise was nowhere to be seen. Neither was Kyle. Many of the fighters who had volunteered were there as well.

My stomach dropped through my boots when I spotted a familiar face. Deirdre, one of the healers, was shambling about, her vacant eyes wide with darkness.

I grabbed Balor's arm and clung on tight, motioning with my other toward the fae. "It's Deirdre. He got to her."

Balor sucked a sharp breath in through his nose, his entire body trembling with rage. "I will kill him."

And so would I. There were several bodies that had fallen to the floor, necks and arms and legs gauged with sharp teeth. Tears pricked my eyes, but I swallowed them down. This sorcerer had taken so many from us. It had to end now.

But where the hell was he?

Glancing around, I saw no sign of a dark magic abuser lurking in the shadows, attempting to control the fight. I'd seen sorcerers only a few times in my life, but they were always distinctive. They wore red, to demonstrate the pact they'd made with magic through their blood. Their soul was forever linked to the power they wielded. When they died, the power would consume the soul to be transformed back into more power.

Some might say they sold their soul to the devil, depending on whether or not you thought magic was evil. I was starting to have my doubts about it myself.

What kind of magic could create things like this? Nothing good, that was for sure.

Besides the red clothing, their hair was usually pure white. The magic sucked out the colour, leaving behind nothing but snowy strands. Their pupils were usually the same. Pretty unnerving, to say the least.

"Try to get everyone out of the way," Balor said to me. "There is one way to end this right here and now, but I need my fae out of harm's way."

I swallowed hard and gave a nod. Balor was going to transform every Sluagh here into nothing but a massive pile of ash.

"Clark?" Balor's voice went rough just as I turned away. I glanced back at him, at the strange emotion churning in his single red eye. "Please be careful. I don't know what I'd do if I lost you to this."

My lips lifted into a smile. "You be careful, too. I might be a little fond of my Prince."

And then we were off, charging through the crowd. Before I could reach any of the fae, I found myself face to face with one of the Sluaghs. Stringy hair, vacant eyes, mouth covered in blood. This one had eaten one of my friends.

With a roar, I lifted my sword and met her steel with my own. It clanged hard, reverberating throughout my entire body. The Sluagh continued on, pulling back and throwing her weight behind her blows. I kept moving. Attack, whirl, kick, slice, punch. No matter what I did, she didn't even flinch.

The world suddenly seemed to slow around me. My senses went sharp. Everything became clearer, like my vision had transformed into super high def. Voices grew louder, and the short puffy breaths of the Sluagh filled my head.

Moving in a strange fluid dance, I ducked and whirled toward the Sluagh. My blade finally made contact, sinking deep into her flesh. A slurping sound rocketed through my skull. I gritted my teeth, forcing myself to keep pushing against the sword until the Sluagh's eyes rolled back into her head.

I ripped out my blade, and her body fell to the ground. I waited for the creature to dissolve into darkness and ash like the vampire Sluagh had in Highgate Cemetery, but nothing happened.

Suddenly, time seemed to zoom back in around me, speeding up again.

I shook my head and moved forward once again, finally reaching Moira and Duncan. They had just finished fighting off their own pair of Sluaghs and were quickly wiping their bloody blades on their trousers.

"Balor said to get everyone to stand back. He's going to burn them."

"He's here?" Duncan's eyes lit up as he scanned the crowd for his Master. He found him, deep within the battle and surrounded by Sluaghs. "Let's get everyone out of the way."

Tipping back his head, Duncan let out a booming battle cry that called to the bond that kept me tethered to my Master. It echoed off the walls, bringing with it a strange force of magic that pounded against my skull. I had to press my hands against my ears at the force of it. But it did the trick. Everyone fell silent, even the Sluaghs. And then the fae began to run.

28

The Sluaghs stumbled after the retreating fae, clearly confused by what was happening. Some began to storm after us, their blades raised high in the air. But they were too slow. They hadn't reacted quickly enough. Balor raised his eye patch. Fire shot through the lobby, engulfing the undead. The blaze was so bright that it hurt my eyes, but I stood there, vowing to watch until every single one of our enemies was gone.

~

There were probably twenty of us that crammed around the door that led into Balor's office. The door was locked and probably barricaded, but that kind of thing really didn't stop Balor the smiter. He didn't even bother to burn it down. All it took was one kick with his powerful leg, and the thing blasted wide open.

Fionn was inside, like we'd expected, standing

quietly behind Balor's oak desk with his hands slung into his pockets. "You're too late. Faerie has already granted me control of this Court. The only way you can get it back is to kill me, and you wouldn't do that. It would tear the entire Court to shreds. Hell, it looks like it's already halfway there already."

"You underestimate me, Fionn," Balor spat. "You always have."

"You would really kill one of your own Masters?" Fionn laughed and shook his head. "Of course you wouldn't. Remember, Balor. I know you. We go back a long way, and I remember what happened when Nemain took over the Silver Court."

I shifted on my feet uneasily, glancing from Balor to Fionn and back again. No one else was in this office with Fionn, and I hadn't seen Tiarnan in the fight. Where was his loyal second? The one he'd used to betray us all?

"Where's Tiarnan?"

Fionn levelled his gaze on me. "He left. It seems you convinced one of my best warriors to decide that Courtless life was better than becoming the heir to the throne."

I snorted. "Heir to the throne. Balor would never name Tiarnan his second."

Fionn's gaze turned to ice. "The first step in my new rule is ridding this Court of the Filthy Carrions within it. As far as I can see, that's just one individual. Clark, I hereby sentence you to death."

Balor roared. He ripped the patch off his eye, and fire shot from deep within his soul. The flames slammed against Fionn. Shocked, I stumbled back. Fionn's mouth opened wide, his eyes bulging out of their sockets. His flesh went black within seconds, and the curdling scream that ripped from his throat would haunt me to my grave.

I closed my eyes and turned away, gritting my teeth against the painful roars. Smoke filled the air, along with the scent of burning flesh. Moira wrapped her arms around my body and pulled me away, out of the room, and down the corridor. I stood there in her arms, shaking, for what felt like days.

∽

I sat in the command station next to Kyle, silently watching him spin through file after file of human reports. Neither one of us said a word. We didn't need to. This Court had been to hell and back, and sometimes quiet was the only way to deal.

It was the middle of the night, but I couldn't sleep. Not with the nightmares that kept plaguing my mind.

The fire. The black flesh.

I would probably never sleep again.

"Would you like a soda?" Kyle asked when he popped a tab on the seventh since I'd curled up in the chair beside him. I shook my head and held up a hand. Caffeine definitely wasn't a great idea for me right now.

He gulped down the soda and tossed the can onto the pile before diving back into his work. After a moment, he stopped and spun in his chair to face me. "You're upset about the burning."

Sometimes, I loved how straight and to the point Kyle was. He kind of just spoke his thoughts out loud, like he had no filter. Not many people were that easy.

It made being around him feel a lot like being at home. That said, I really didn't want to talk about the burning.

I didn't even want to think about it ever again.

"I mean, it was pretty horrific, Kyle."

"You've seen Balor burn things before."

"Things." I wrapped my arms around my knees and hugged them to my chest. "Buildings. Sluaghs. Not living, breathing creatures. He killed someone, Kyle. And not just any someone. A member of his own Court. A Master of one of his Houses. Besides the horror of it all, it is going to cause a lot of problems. I don't think any of us are ready for it, especially not when a sorcerer keeps attacking us with Sluaghs."

"You're right. It's going to suck." He tucked a pen behind his ear and peered out at me from underneath his mess of curls. "How much do you know about the death sentencing magic?"

"Is it like the whole traitor thing? Stripping a fae's power and feeding them to the Sluaghs?" I gave a nod. "Yeah, it freaked me out, but—"

"No. That's what happens when Faerie as a whole deems you a traitor. Princes also carry the power to sentence someone to death, if they deem it necessary. Usually, they won't do that unless the accused is brought before a trial of their own peers, but Fionn was likely feeling desperate."

"What are you trying to say?"

"Basically, Fionn gave you the curse of death. It's one of the only curses that fae can wield." Kyle shrugged. "There's no breaking it, not without a different payment of death. *Fionn's* death. If Balor hadn't killed him when he did, you would have died within twenty-four hours."

I blinked at him, suddenly wishing he had some gin in that neverending pile of drinks. "Are you serious?"

"You can look it up." Kyle passed a book over to me from a pile next to his desk. "In fact, you should probably read this thing. It includes a lot of important information about how the Court works. I think it talks about death sentences in chapter sixty-eight."

"Thanks, Kyle." I brushed my finger against the knobby leather cover. "So, you're saying…Balor killed Fionn because it was the only way to save my life?"

"Pretty much. So, if I were you, I probably wouldn't be weird with him about it next time you see him. In order to save you, he did something that's probably going to screw us all."

Biggest understatement of the year.

~

After that, I paced the halls for at least two hours. I had to think. I had to breathe. And I needed to walk off some of my nervous energy. I had finally made it back to my room and had thrown the covers over my body just as a heavy knock sounded on my door. Frowning, I peered at the clock. It was two in the bloody morning. Too late for a mission and way too early for training. Sighing, I threw my feet over the edge of the bed and padded to the door.

When I opened it, I found Balor leaning heavily against the wooden frame and staring down at me with an expression so weary that he almost looked like he was about to pass out. I wanted nothing more than to scoop him up in my arms and hold onto him forever.

"Are you busy?"

I looked down at my matching fox pajamas and back at my bed, but then I said, "No."

"Good. Kyle just got a hit on a possible location for the sorcerer, and I need you to come with me to check it out."

"Okay. Where is he?"

Balor pressed his lips together. "The Tower of London."

"Oh." My eyes widened. That made sense with Caer's prophecy. A place of death. That was the Tower of London, alright. Or, it had been, once upon a time. "What did Kyle find?"

"Some tourists complaining about some realistic zombies wandering around the tunnels. Freaked them out. One of them got clawed in the face. Her skin got infected. Two days later, she died."

"This is sounding plausible."

He closed his eye. "Do you think you're up for this?"

"Of course I'm up for this. We've been searching for this sorcerer for days. He just attacked our Court. I'm done waiting for something to happen. We need to go find him and put a stop to this once and for all."

"That's not what I mean, Clark. And you know it." He sucked in a deep breath, eye still closed, almost as if he couldn't bear to see my expression. "Are you up for doing this? After what happened? After what you saw me do?"

"Balor." I reached up and placed my hand against

his face. His eye cracked open, and I took a slow step toward him until my chest was pressed tight against his. I gazed up at my Prince and smiled. "I know why you did what you did, and I do not blame you. If anything, I blame Fionn. We have a lot of trouble coming our way, but it isn't your fault. It's his. And I'll be here by your side no matter what comes our way."

Balor leaned down and kissed me roughly. I clutched his shirt, pressing up onto my toes to get as close to him as I could. After a moment, he pulled back, cheeks flushed with colour. "Just that once. I needed to kiss you, just that once."

But then he kissed me again.

29

We stood outside the Tower of London with as many fae as we'd been able to gather. Balor stood in front with Duncan and Moira flanking each side. Cormac, me, and a dozen other fighters clustered behind our Master. The other willing fighters had been left back at Court. We couldn't leave our House unprotected, not after everything that had happened.

It was well past midnight, and a bulbous moon hung low in the sky, half-obscured by bloated grey clouds. A light fog had settled across London's streets, wisps of white smoke drifting across the ancient towers that rose up before us. There were no tourists, but the royal guards would still be inside. Several lived inside the Tower, keeping an eye on things day and night.

Of course, that didn't explain why the black gate was cracked open.

"Come on." Balor motioned for us to follow him. "Be on guard. We don't know exactly what we're going to find in here."

Moira and Duncan moved ahead of Balor and pushed open the large gate that spanned the distance between two bulbous towers. It kept visitors locked out and the Crown Jewels locked in. At one point in time, hundreds and hundreds of years ago, this place had been used to house prisoners and was consumed by torture and death. Because of this, it was rumoured to be one of the most haunted places in Britain.

The sorcerer had chosen such a lovely, happy place to build his Army of the Dead.

The gates clanged open, and we all filed through the majestic archway. Balor took the lead again, taking us over a bridge and through another archway. Once inside, our boots scuffed against the ancient cobblestone of the outer ward, a series of roads that ran along the outer edge of the Tower. The sky had grown darker, and deep shadows clung to every corner. Balor curled his hand into a fist, and that bright sparkling magic flickered across his fingers, illuminating our surroundings.

The cobblestone road stretched out before us, cutting through the inner and outer walls that once served as protection for this place. In the distance, the Wakefield Tower rose high, the chambers of kings who had long since died. In one of the small cross-shaped windows, orange light flickered from within.

Unease skittered down my spine. "Everyone else see that?"

Murmurs of agreement surrounded me. None of my fellow fighters seemed particularly excited about our findings. The sorcerer had proven tricky so far. There was no telling what we would find inside.

We made our way toward the tower as quietly as

possible. Not a single one of us said a word, and our footsteps were light even against the stone ground. Finally, we reached the entrance. It was, as the others had been, open.

"I'll go first," Balor said. "Stay close behind me. Once inside, do what I say. No questions asked."

I knew none of us liked this one little bit. We all had the instinct to protect our Prince, to stand in front of him rather than behind. But he'd given his order. Based on the magic shuddering against my skin, it was one that would stick.

Balor took the lead, taking us through a maze of large rooms, decorated with beds and medieval furniture to show tourists how queens and kings had once lived in this expansive space. Balor kept moving, quickly, through the rooms, and I knew why.

The sound of scuttling had reached my ears. It was growing louder, echoing against the stone walls. Somewhere up ahead, we would find the Sluaghs.

We trailed up a curving staircase and stopped on the skinny landing when we finally saw what was waiting for us. Just up ahead in an oval room with curving vaulted stone ceilings, a man in a red cloak sat lounging on a throne. He had his hands folded neatly in his lap, and one leg casually tossed over the other. His pale hair was thin at the top, but his moustache was thick and bountiful. Ageing lines stretched out from his eyes and lips, but even with all the wrinkles, he didn't look a day over thirty.

I curled my free hand into a fist and narrowed my eyes.

"Ah." He smiled, opening up his strange, unnerving eyes that were the colour of the whitest clear-day clouds. "Our guests have finally joined us then. Welcome. I am Eoin, sorcerer of London. I have been waiting for you."

A Sluagh shambled over to him from the right. She was one of as many as thirty undead crammed into the small space. She handed the sorcerer a small flickering torch about the size of a pencil. That was when I realised, the whole place reeked of petrol.

"Come on inside," he said again, with a wide smile. "If you do not, I will drop this torch, and all of you will die."

The arsehole had done it again.

We all stood tense in the thin corridor just outside of the throne room, waiting for Balor's order. After several long moments, he gave a nod.

"Let's go."

As we began to move inside, the sorcerer held up the torch again. "Just so we're all clear here. If you make any move against me or mine, I will drop this torch. So, you best do as I say."

Narrowing my eyes, I glared at the sorcerer as we all eased inside the room. A large metal chandelier hung low overhead. On it sat about twenty blood red candles, all lit up with flames. This sorcerer really was insane. With the petrol on the floor, all it would take was one wrong drip of wax, and we'd all be dead.

When we had all shuffled into the center of the room, the door slammed shut behind us. I turned to watch a Sluagh slide the bolt into place. We were trapped. There were two large windows to the left of the throne, but they were clearly locked tight, and it would be a drop to the stone ground below.

"Right," Balor said, striding forward, his body

rippling in barely controlled anger. "What is it that you want?"

The sorcerer laughed and leaned back into the white granite throne. "Shouldn't I be the one asking that question? You're the one who came to me."

"I came here because I want to put a stop to you attacking my Court." Balor sneered. "Your turn. What do you want?"

"I thought I made myself clear in my note. I want every supernatural to die, starting with your Court."

I narrowed my eyes. This guy was clearly insane. Whatever magic he'd tapped into for his powers had driven him to madness.

"Why?" Balor asked. "What is the point of all this?"

"Easy." Eoin used one hand to grip the arm of the throne and sat up straight. "I wish to rule."

Balor let out a harsh laugh. "You can kill every single one of us in London, but Faerie will never let a sorcerer rule a Court."

"Oh, I don't mean your Court. I couldn't care less about that." He leaned forward, his white eyes flashing against the light of the torch. "I will rule the *humans*. With no other supernaturals in my way, they will turn to me. I will take England's throne for my own."

I snorted. I couldn't help myself. I'd never heard such egotistical madness in my life.

His strange white eyes cut my way. "Is there a problem?"

"Yeah, I don't think I'm the one who has the problem," I said. "I mean, you do realise the monarchy isn't quite the same thing it was hundreds of years ago, right? It's mostly ceremonial now. If you wanted to take control of England, your best bet would have been running for Prime Minister, not trying to steal a crown from an old woman everyone loves."

"The monarchy doesn't operate with tyranny *now*," Eoin said, clutching his torch tight in his trembling hand. "But it will once I am through with it."

Yeah, okay, you muppet. I rolled my eyes. Honestly, I really couldn't take this guy seriously.

"You do also realise that the throne you're sitting on is a replica meant for tourists, right? It's not actually a throne that any king has sat on."

"Enough!" His voice boomed against the stone walls. Even the Sluaghs shifted on their feet in response. "Any more words from you, and I will drop this torch."

He didn't want to drop the torch. I could see it in his eyes. But he was so far gone into crazy land that he'd probably do it anyway.

"Now." The sorcerer pushed up from the fake throne and strode down the steps. "You are all going to do exactly as I say, or we're all going to die. None of you want that, do you?"

Balor let out a low growl, but he didn't say a word.

"Good." Eoin smiled. "First up, I'd like…you to come here."

He pointed at Alastair, one of the fighters who had volunteered to join us on this mission. He was tall and muscular with silver hair that he wore pushed back from his angular face. The fae frowned at the sorcerer but threw back his shoulders and strode forward, showing no sign of cowardice. My heart thumped as I watched the sorcerer slowly round Alastair, drinking in his strong biceps, the slant of his jaw, and the brilliant silver hair that sat in jagged chunks on top of his head.

Eoin closed his eyes and began to mutter. His voice was low, melodic, and held a darkness that sounded as though it were coming straight from his blackened soul. Strange electricity shot through the stone room. A tunnel of wind began to build. It surrounded the sorcerer and Alastair until I could see nothing other than a tornado of dark power that consumed them both.

Suddenly, the wind stopped, sucking all the air out of the room along with it. I panted hard at the sudden change in pressure, but forced myself to hold my ground.

Eoin was standing there just as he had before, only his bright white eyes were now open. He gazed strangely, and curiously, at Alastair's face.

Alastair's silver eyes were now dark and hollow. When he turned to us, it was clear that the brave fighter I'd met only days before was now gone. My stomach flipped over itself, and my hands curled into fists. We had just witnessed something I'd never in a million years wanted to see.

Eoin had turned Alastair into a Sluagh.

"That is enough." Balor stormed toward Eoin, but the sorcerer held up the torch, smiling broadly. Balor stopped short, but he kept his hand tight around the hilt of his sword.

"Don't tempt me to drop this torch. Because I *will* do it."

I shifted closer to Moira, our shoulders forming a strengthening bond between us. There had to be something we could do. Not only to undo what the sorcerer had just done but to stop him from doing it to anyone else. It was clear now why he'd lured us here. He planned to turn us all into Sluaghs.

And it seemed Balor was on the same wavelength as me.

"Perhaps I will let you turn us all to ash," Balor said in a low growl. "You plan to kill us all anyway with your Sluagh curse. Being burnt alive might be painful, but being turned into a Sluagh is much worse."

"There is where you're wrong," the sorcerer said, waving the torch back and forth like a taunt. "My grimoire explains how to undo the curse. Maybe, just maybe, if you do what I say and fight for me like the good little Sluagh you'll be, I'll turn you back. You'll be in decent shape. After a lot of experimenting, I have found a way to keep Sluaghs from disintegrating above ground. I got it wrong a few times. Some of them kept turning into dark skeletons and crumbling ashy things. But I've fixed it now. You're welcome."

Balor froze. I knew exactly what he was thinking. Hell, I was thinking it, too. We needed that damn book. Turning Maeve back into the regular fae that she was wouldn't completely solve all our problems, but it would help. There would be only one dead Master then instead of two.

Of course, we had to somehow avoid getting turned into Sluaghs before we could manage that.

"Good. Next up," Eoin said, scanning our group. His white bulbous eyes stopped right on me. And then they shifted to where my shoulder was linked with Moira's. "Her. The warrior looking one. She'll make a nice addition to my army."

"No." My voice cracked. I grabbed onto Moira's arm, keeping her tight to my side. I glanced at my friend, at her bright golden hair and eyes full of defiant fire. Even if there was a spell to undo the curse, I would not let this sorcerer take her away from me.

"It wasn't a question." The sorcerer sneered. He held a hand out toward Moira, waited.

"I will not let you do this to her." My heart had begun to pound in my ears, blood rushing through my head so thick and so fast that I could barely think around it.

"You have no other choice, Filthy Carrion." He spat the words, but for once, they did not make me cringe. They only amplified my growing rage, my building fear. Suddenly, the world around me went razor sharp. Colours went vibrant, details were larger than life.

My eyes had shifted.

I curled my lips into a smile at the look of shock on the sorcerer's face.

"Careful, Clark," I heard Balor's voice murmur as if it were inside of my head.

But his words did little to calm me. I could feel the magic of his order whisper across my skin, and the bond between us snapped tight. For once, it did little to contain me. I could feel it there, calling to me, begging me to give in. But something much more primal now buzzed across my skin.

So, I cast the order aside.

The sorcerer's smug smile faltered. "Let go of her now, or I will drop it."

I didn't let go.

Moira shifted by my side and dropped her mouth to my ear. "Clark, calm down. Maybe you should just let me go. Better one of us than all of us, eh?"

My soul felt ripped in half. She was just giving up. She was just going to let this sorcerer turn her into a mindless member of the walking dead. I clutched on tighter to her arm, but she calmly began to pry my fingers off her skin.

And then the sorcerer lunged.

He reached out to grab Moira away from me. His hand wrapped around her arm, and he tugged. Between my half-pried fingers, and his surprising strength, Moira flew out of my grasp.

Rage and fear churned through me. I bent over, clutched my knees, and vomited on the floor. Everything around me buzzed. My vision went so blurry that I could barely see. The floor tilted beneath me, and I fell hard onto my knees. Sobs shook through my body, and the sound of a million flapping wings filled my head.

Glass crashed.

I glanced up from where I heaved to see dozens of black birds—ravens—pouring through the broken window. They swarmed toward the sorcerer who had dropped his grip on Moira's arm. His eyes widened as they flew for him, over our heads and straight toward his face.

The first bird reached him and pecked its dark beak right into the sorcerer's eye. Blood spurted from his face. His gurgle screamed ripped through the room, echoing again and again off the stone.

I pushed up from the floor, mouth ajar.

What the hell was happening?

And then the sorcerer dropped the torch.

I screamed, diving toward the flaming stick, hands outstretched. But a small winged creature soared down and grasped the stick with its claws. It grabbed the torch when it was only centimetres from making contact with the floor. And then the bird whooshed away, back out into the night.

Dozens of ravens had now landed on the sorcerer. They were pecking at his face, at his arms, and at his legs. His blood splattered the stone floor, his gurgled screams dropping away as he collapsed, dead, on the ground.

The birds were gone just as quickly as they'd come. They left behind nothing more than a barely recognisable corpse. We all stared at it, shocked. I didn't think any of us understood exactly what had just happened.

Somehow, we'd been saved by the ravens of the Tower of London.

Balor dragged his hand down his face. "Right. Well, that's done. The sorcerer is dead."

I met Moira's eyes across the room, and she gave me a relieved smile. Thank the heavens. She was safe. We were all safe.

"What exactly happened, boss?" Duncan asked. "Where did those ravens come from? And why did they attack him but not us?"

"There have been ravens at the Tower of London for as long as I can remember. I never thought they had any supernatural origin, but maybe they do." He shrugged. "Maybe they've been protecting this place all along. They sensed a threat, and they got rid of it."

We all turned to look at the bloody body on the ground.

"Erm, I hate to point this out," Cormac said, pointing a shaking finger at the cluster of Sluaghs that had started shambling toward us. "But we've got a ton of undead we still haven't dealt with."

Undead who were clearly not attacking us.

Balor turned toward the Sluaghs. He approached the nearest, Alastair, who was swaying on his feet, staring dumbly at something none of us could see. He was acting a hell of a lot like Maeve, and so were the others. We all filtered through the crowd, giving each one a good look. None of them were attacking us, and they were all clearly previous supernaturals: shifters, vampires, and fae.

I trailed over to the throne while the rest of the guards discussed our next steps. An old, dusty tome had been shoved between the wall and the throne. I pulled it out, blew the dust off the top. It was the sorcerer's grimoire. Inside, we would find the spell to remove the curse.

Balor's eyes caught mine, and he gave me a nod. "Alright, this is what we're going to do. We need to get a boat, and then we'll smuggle these poor creatures out of here through the Traitor's Gate. We'll keep them in the catacombs until we can find another sorcerer who can undo the curse."

30

I knocked on the door of Balor's penthouse. He'd asked to see me after we'd returned from a long night of ferrying the dead from the Tower of London to the West Norwood catacombs. It had taken us hours, but we'd managed to get it done before the morning guards arrived.

Balor opened the door, smiled, and ushered me inside. He'd taken a shower, and his silver-streaked hair was still damp. Small flecks of water had dripped onto his tight, black shirt, and it was all I could do not to rub my fingers across the droplets.

He shut the door behind me and motioned for me to sit on the sofa while he made me a gin and tonic, just how I liked it. When he handed it to me, I took the cool drink greedily in my hands. It might be before noon, but I needed it after the night we'd had.

He poured a whiskey for himself and eased into the armchair, sighing loudly as he let his muscular body relax into the leather. "So."

"So." I took a sip.

"We managed to do it. Sometimes, I think we're a good team."

I arched a brow. "Only sometimes?"

A ghost of a smile flickered across his face. "Other times, we have a tendency to get on each other's nerves."

"You're not wrong about that." I set down my drink and brought out the crimson skull I'd taken from the vampire's shop. "I have something for you."

Balor leaned forward, a strange smile on his face. He took the skull, turned it over. "You got me a skull cauldron?"

My lips twitched. "It reminded me of your throne."

He chuckled, stood, and placed it in the middle of a shelf just beside a golden picture frame. It held a photo of himself and the Princess who had led the Silver Court before Nemain killed her and took it for herself.

Frowning, I glanced away. "Why did you want to see me?"

I had a feeling it had something to do with my whole freak-out at the Tower. Not only had I shifted my eyes, but I'd completely ignored his order, without any help from alcohol to numb my mind. I had also totally lost my head, what with the whole vomiting and crashing to my knees thing.

"Your fae powers are growing stronger," he said, striding back over to the armchair and sinking in. He took another sip of his drink. "And so is your shifter side. That has some interesting repercussions."

"You think that's why I was able to ignore your order?"

"I do." A beat passed. "While I understand your strong emotions in that situation, we do need to work on developing some better control."

"Because you don't want me to be able to say no to you."

"That is not why, Clark." Balor set down his glass, stood, and joined me on the sofa. He was sitting far enough away that another fae could have squished between us, but the closeness still made every muscle in my body clench tight. His scent enveloped me, jasmine, moss, and vanilla. "I want you to be able to control it for your own safety. It has nothing to do with our bond. You were two seconds away from launching yourself at the sorcerer, and it could have gotten you killed."

"It could have gotten us all killed," I whispered. "I know, and I'm sorry. I just…"

"Shifters are known for having volatile emotions. It's only normal, Clark. But we need to get a handle on it."

I glanced up, meeting his fiery gaze. My stomach flipped. He was everything I wanted, and the one thing I could never have. Even if *he* one day decided to ignore the prophecy so that he could take me as his, I, on the other hand, would never be able to do it.

I could never let myself become the thing that got him killed.

As if reading every thought passing through my mind, his smile faltered. "I know, Clark. I know." He took my hand in his and squeezed. "I wish there was some other way."

We were no longer talking about my shifter side now.

"Caer's prophecies tend to come true, don't they?" I asked.

"They always come true."

"Is there a way to change them? Is there a way to alter the future so that they can't come true?"

He flicked his gaze down, and then back up at me. "I have been searching for a way to change her prophecy for twenty years, Clark. And I have found nothing."

My heart thumped hard, and slowly, Balor pulled his hand away. "But I did not call you here for that, nor did I call you here to discuss your shifter side. I wanted to warn you about what's to come. You're new to the Court. You might not understand the consequences of these past few days."

"Fionn."

He gave a nod. "Yes, Fionn. His House will blame me for his death, and rightly so. His second, which is no longer Tiarnan, will take over as Master. His name is Aed, and he is a harsher critic than Fionn ever was. Things are going to get worse here in the Crimson Court before they get better." He took my hand once again and held it tightly against his chest. "So, I am going to ask you once again. Are you certain you wish to stay?"

"This Court has become my home," I said without any hesitation at all. "I'm not going anywhere, and I'll do everything I can to help. Bring on the next fight for the throne."

Thank you for reading *Dead Fae Walking*, the second book in The Paranormal PI Files. Curious about Clark's first meeting with Balor? You can grab the prequel story for free by signing up to my reader newsletter.

Bad Fae Rising, the third book in the series, launches April 24th and is available for preorder on Amazon.

ABOUT THE AUTHOR

Jenna Wolfhart is a Buffy-wannabe who lives vicariously through the kick-ass heroines in urban fantasy. After completing a PhD in Librarianship, she became a full-time author and now spends her days typing the fantastical stories in her head. When she's not writing, she loves to stargaze, binge Netflix, and drink copious amounts of coffee.

Born and raised in America, Jenna now lives in England with her husband, her dog, and her mischief of rats.

FIND ME ONLINE
Facebook Reader Group
Instagram
YouTube
Twitter

www.jennawolfhart.com
jenna@jennawolfhart.com

Printed in Great Britain
by Amazon